www.FifthAveEnt.com

Fifth Avenue Entertainment
P.O.Box 146
Suite 210
Flowery Branch GA 30542
www.FifthAveEnt.com

Printed in the United States of America

First Edition: November 2010

10 9 8 7 6 5 4 3 2 1

ISBN-13: 978-1-9357562-5-5
ISBN-10: 1-9357562-5-7

Cover design by: Charles "Chase" Preston
Cover photograph: Tolga Kavut

Lisa's Acknowledgements

I started this journey a while ago; I got sidetracked with other obligations in my life. Yet, here we are. I want to first thank my Lord and savior JESUS CHRIST. I am here through GOD's grace and Mercy. I believe that my steps are ordered and everything that has happened in my life--the good, the bad and the ugly was allowed. I am who I am because of every experience. I believe that things happen when they are suppose to so, here we are.

Miasha & Rich- Thank you for the opportunity. It is a pleasure to work with you both. I look forward to our many projects. I adore you two and glad that we've become good friends. Thank you for the laughs. And we thought this connection was just about working out, Lol. They are not ready!

ED- Your unwavering support is everything! Thanks for knowing when to change hats. I love you.

Jordan, Justin and EJ-The best sons a mother could ask for. I am so proud and honored to be your mother. I love you with everything that is within me.

Mom- Your unconditional love and support means the world to me and your jokes provide laughter at the right time. I love you so much.

Dad- Your patience, compassion and love have given me balance. You are my hero. I love you Daddy.

Sherrie-We should have been twins. We are so in sync with one another. I love you and wish we could be together every day. Every day is like a party when we are together. I love you big sis!

Andre- My ride or die. Need I say more? I love you and I believe in you.

Stanley & Jay-You two are so much alike. I love your hearts and your spirit. You two are wonderful! I love you big Brothers.

Carlos-Thanks for heading up the fan club Lol. I love you and appreciate all of your support.

Marlowe- Thank you for just being you. Love you sis!

Tyler Perry-Your determination, drive and Vision inspire me. I remember fifteen years ago you telling me what you were going to do and how you were going to do it. It blows me away. I am inspired. I love you.

Thank you for being a real friend.

The rest of my family and dear friends, Mom Hartwell, Pops, Rosie, Johanna, Eric, Nona, Derrick, Jimmy, Uncle Cliff, Jenny, Alice, Maya, Kendra, April, Warren, Zack, Tammie, Elita, Cecil, Sandy, Fred, Oscar, Auntee & Unc, Nene, Karon, the entire Thompson family, Rhonda, Princess, Joye C., Roger Bobb, Jonell, Carlos, Hinton, Karen G, Angie, Katrina, Lacheri, Leslie, Sheree B., Mark H., Jamal, Kenya, Angela and Essence Magazine Thank you for all of your support! I love you.

Alpha Tyler- Thank you for believing in me.

Eva Stancil and Margo Gabriel-Lets get it!

Mimi- I love you. They don't come better than you. You're up next! I love you.

My girls back home- Nay, Myra, Mi Esha, Crystal P., Inga, Janene, Pam, Tika, Anita, Crystal L.--You guys have provided an abundance of laughs and inspiration for many books and movies to come. I love you all.

The Wus, The Kingis, The Reeses, The Gordons, Mays, Savoys, and Riveras -- I love you!

My boys back home- Danei, Justin, Keith R., Keith M., Darren, Gabe, David, Giant, Kenny, Vic, Jason, Chris, Kevin, Charles, Fred, William, Thank you for all the Laughs! When's the next bagging session?

My Glam squad-Pairra Thomas, Elijah Cohen, Windell Boutee, Sergio Hudson, Lamar, Kidada, I love you! Thanks for providing the Wow factor.

Sterling, Janay, Alex- thanks for being my #1 fans. I love u dearly.

To all of my fans-I appreciate your support! I look forward to meeting each one of you.

And to anyone I may have missed, please charge it to my head and not my heart.

Peace and Blessings! XOXOXO

Lisa

Miasha's Acknowledgements

This has been such a trying time in my life and to think I managed to write a book with Lisa Wu Hartwell and put it out is a miracle. I only have Allah to thank for the will power, creativity, and resources.

My family—immediate, distant and in between, my appreciation to you for all you do to hold me down and lift me up. You play a huge part in my success.

Rich and the two most important lil' men to me, Amir and Ace, I love and admire you so much. Thank you for making my home life so content. At the end of the day you keep me sane and grounded and remind me of what's really important in this life.

Aunt Wanda and Uncle Jimmy, for coming through for me on so many levels. You two have had my back for a lonnnng time. Can't wait to return the favor.

Mommy and Daddy, Every book, every accomplishment you two are right there rooting me on. And it is a reminder of how far you two have come. I love you both beyond words and can't express how grateful I am for having you in my life during these times.

My friends, it's rare to find people like you these days. So glad I found yall way back when. Love yall much and still waiting for that out-door lunch!

Aunt Merrie for being a part of this project! Look at you proofreading a Miasha & Lisa Wu Hartwell book! Go girl! Lol

My fans, you already know what it is. You are my lifeline. Point, blank, period. Thank you for keeping me going.

Thank you sincerely, Hakim at Black and Nobel, for your advice and encouragement. And all the bookstores, distributors, and vendors, for embracing this collaboration, thank you!

My creative team, Chase Preston and Tolga Kavut, for understanding my vision and making it happen. Liza Dawson, for your insight and input.

A very special person, Karen E. Quinones Miller for giving me the push, pull, and everything else I could have possibly needed to get this done and get it done Right! You are amazing! I pray everyday to be half the person you are. Love you, lady!

Another very special person, Rich, this thanks is for being a supportive and stand-up partner and teammate. Your 50% is very much appreciated!

To Lisa Wu & Ed Hartwell, this has been quite the connection. Thanks for the opportunity and all the fun times! This is just the beginning, can you believe it?

And to everybody else who continuously play a part in my success, career, life, or any aspect of who I am and what I do, thank you. You mean a lot to me!

Ya Girl,

Minsh

This book is dedicated to the Men in my life:
Ed, Jordan, Justin & EJ -

Ed, thank you for loving me unconditionally and being a wonderful husband and friend. I love you.

My three sons . . . I love you more than you could possibly imagine. You keep my heart beating.

In loving memory of
Oscar "Meho" Brislis

Lisa Wu Hartwell

Sheryl

I was walking into Bel Air Presbyterian, a massive Los Angeles church that was attended by countless Hollywood stars every Sunday.

My entourage of distant family members and one life long best friend accompanied me. Ramona, my best friend since elementary school, was holding the lengthy 7 ½ foot train of my off-white charmeuse Vera Wang wedding gown. My adopted mother was holding my left hand, carefully guiding my every step. Then there was someone lightly stroking loose strands of my hair back in place. And a fourth person kept repeating, "Don't cry. Just hold off. You don't wanna ruin your beautiful make-up."

That, I didn't. But it was hard to hold back tears; my emotions were beginning to get the best of me. Realizing that I was about to marry a man who had given me more love and affection in the past year that we'd been dating than my ex-husband had given me in the thirteen years we'd been married. I was overwhelmed with happiness and a sense of freedom. It had been a long time since I felt true companionship from a man that didn't come with verbal, physical, and sexual abuse. I didn't know how to act.

"You ready, Sheryl?" Ramona asked.

I smiled and nodded. She smiled back, and took her place in the line of seven women who made up my bridal party. My adopted sister Liz was my maid of honor, and she stood in the front of the line; stoic and poised. Her tall, slender frame gave her the appearance of a runway model and her smooth, mocha skin and long straight hair put her Caribbean roots on display. Behind her was Ramona, the one woman in the bunch I was actually close to. She and I remained tight as I was shuffled from foster home to foster home until I was finally adopted. Even over the past thirteen years she remained in contact, despite my ex's attempts at keeping me isolated from anyone who really gave a damn about me. The other five women in the bridal party consisted of an aunt, a cousin, and three of my husband-to-be's relatives. We had to put them in the wedding so that all the groomsmen would have someone to walk down the aisle with. My husband had a lot of friends and a big family.

The pianist began playing *Canon in D Major* by German Baroque composer Johann Pachelbel, and the violinists joined in. Butterflies began fluttering in my stomach as I listened for the vocalists' first word. That would be my cue.

My arm wrapped in my father's, I took a deep breath, fought back tears, and got ready to meet the new love of my life at the altar.

But before I could take my first step down the aisle, I heard whispers coming from behind me. I turned around as one of the ushers murmured, "Somebody just pulled up. Do you want to wait?"

I glanced out the stained glass window to see who it was just arriving to my wedding. But the truth of the matter was I didn't care. I was not going to wait; I was too anxious. So anxious that I was totally oblivious to the fact that it was my ex-husband's car that had pulled up and parked outside the church. Why he came, I wished I would never have had to find out.

Leslie

"**W**here the fuck is he? Where the fuck is he?" I paced the back office in a fury. "Somebody get me another cigarette, please!"

"Have a seat, Les. Good Lord. You're gonna give us all a heart attack," my grandmother yapped in her heavy Italian accent.

"Grandma, Frank is supposed to be kissing the bride right now and he's not even here! He's not picking up his phone! Nothing! How am I supposed to sit down at a time like this? Could you sit down if this were you?"

"I'm in a wheelchair, of course!"

I huffed at my grandmother's sarcasm, this was not the time for her bullshit.

"Besides, you know his kind is always late," she snarled. "What do the Blacks call it? CP time?"

"Enough!" I all but shouted. I couldn't take her insults anymore. Here I was at my dream wedding at the Lladros boutique on Rodeo Drive, in my dream dress, a vintage Chanel by Karl Lagerfield, in front of five hundred people who all doubted this day would come, and my groom is a got damn no-show! I was angry beyond words and didn't think I could get any angrier. It was then that my younger sister barged in the office with news of my husband-to-be's whereabouts.

"I found Frank," she said.

"Thank heavens, Renee. Where's the son-of-a-bitch? Let's get this wedding going," my grandmother almost shouted.

"He's at Cedars-Sinai," my sister said, glancing first at my grandmother then landing her eyes on me.

"Why is he at the hospital? What happened?" I asked, suddenly shocked and worried.

My sister's face grew long and her big brown eyes lowered as she began to explain.

My heart dropped. I didn't know what to expect. I finally took a seat like my grandmother suggested.

"I don't know how to tell you this, Leslie, but," my sister took a deep breath, "his wife just gave birth to their third child."

I didn't react right away because what my sister had just said didn't register right away. I was trying to make sure I heard her correctly before I said anything.

"A boy or a girl?" my grandmother asked.

"A girl," my sister responded, still with the puppy dog eyes.

And that's when it hit me.

"Are you fucking kidding me?" I snapped. "That sleazy motherfucker! He said, he *promised* it was over between them! He divorced her once and for fucking all and gave me the wedding I demanded! Allowed me to plan it everyday of my life for the last eleven months, all the while he was making a baby with her?!" I started breathing heavily. My temper blasted through the roof of Lladros. I jumped up out of the chair and stormed out of the room.

"Where are you going?" My sister was right behind me.

I didn't answer. Instead I jabbed the down button on the elevator.

"Where are you going?"

"I need a cigarette," I said, momentarily taking my anger out on the down button. "Fuck it." I headed to the stairs.

I picked up my dress and marched down the winding stairs adorned with a red carpet that was supposed to serve as my wedding aisle. My guests, who had been seated on the main floor of the high-end figurine boutique for a whole two hours, all looked up at me as I approached their level. The 'I told you so' looks on their faces fueled me even more. The pastor, who was now sitting at the altar rather than standing like he had been when it was time for the ceremony to start an hour and a half ago, hopped up and started toward me -- confusion written all over his face.

"What's going on?" I heard him ask.

I kept walking; heading out the front door.

My sister stopped, I guessed to tell the pastor the situation, and that gave me just enough time to hail a cab and disappear before she or anybody could talk me out of what I was about to do.

"Take me to Holmby Hills, please."

The cabby asked no questions. He just took off, en route to Frank's Tudor-style mansion.

I was more than disgusted when we pulled up to the mansion; there were pink balloons that read 'It's a Girl' tied to a stork planted in his front yard. No cars were in the driveway and all six garages were closed, which usually meant no one was home.

"Stay right here, I'll go get your money," I told the cab driver.

I climbed out of the backseat, walked over to the iron gates, punched the code in the box, and was granted entry to the gates which led to what was supposed to be my permanent home in seven days.

I turned back to look at the driver and held up my finger, signaling him to wait. I didn't want him following me down Frank's driveway. I needed to release my anger without any interference.

I walked to Frank's front door and entered yet another code. The door opened. I went in and entered a third code to shut the alarm off. *How dare he do this to me*, I said to myself. *He must think I'm a damn fool.*

I went downstairs to the basement and retrieved Frank's eight-year old son's baseball bat, then went into the garages -- one at a time -- and pretended like Frank's collection of exotic and luxury cars were him. I started by busting out the windows of each and every one of them. Then I beat on the hoods and doors, front lights and rear lights. The alarms were going off, like crazy but that didn't stop me. I was in a zone.

Angie

"So we're all set to begin. Are you excited?" Deb, the mid-forties TV show producer, asked.

Grinning, I nodded.

"All right, good. I'm gonna get everybody in place. I'll send your dad in in a sec."

"Okay," I murmured.

"I can't believe you're going through with this, Angie," Deidre, my massage therapist and friend, expressed as she zipped the back of my gown. "I mean, you've only known this man, what, six months? And on top of that, you don't even know . . ."

"Shhh," I stopped her when I saw my father entering the room.

"Wow." My father's toothless smile almost brought me to tears. "You look absolutely beautiful, my daughter."

"Awww. Thank you, daddy."

"Hi, Mr. Wayne." Deidre greeted my father with a hug.

"Hey there, Deidre."

"Well, daddy, I'm all ready to get hitched."

"I see, I see. I sure wish your mother could be here for this. She always talked about what her only daughter's wedding day would be like."

"Daddy, you're gonna make me cry. Please stop."

"Okay, okay." My dad pulled me in for a hug.

Over his shoulder I peeped at Deidre. Her lips were twisted as she rolled her eyes. She shook her head and mouthed, "Don't do this."

The producer popped in. "It's show time."

I pulled away from my dad and dabbed the corners of my eyes. Meanwhile Deidre slid past us to take her seat among the four hundred plus spectators. My dad and I interlocked arms as we walked out of the beach house and onto the sand.

The live band began to play the instrumental of the traditional wedding song, 'Here Comes The Bride.' The guests rose to their feet and turned their attention to my father and me. I saw a lot of familiar faces, and just as many unfamiliar faces. There were cameras everywhere. It seemed every major media outlet was present. There was even a helicopter hovering above. The crew from the TV show, 'Million Dollar Marriages', which my groom hosted, was dispersed in their positions with cameras, sound booms, and lights. It was a spectacle.

The weather was pleasant; not too hot yet nowhere near cold. The ocean was at its bluest and waves were calm. The over-sized plexi-glass plank that was custom-built on top of the water supported rows upon rows of chairs draped in white luxurious seat covers with satin bows tied at the backs. Exotic flowers, flown in from all parts of the world, decorated a large and gorgeous arch at the end of the aisle. Through the arch all you could see was the endless ocean. It was beautiful.

I was a little nervous about stepping onto the plank - - I wasn't a swimmer and walking on water didn't sit so comfortably with me – but for the sake of the production I would be gutsy. In fact, it was for the sake of the production that this wedding was happening in the first place. I never in a million years saw myself getting married, let alone to a man whom I had just met. But it was like it was out of my control. One minute I went out to dinner with Bobby Fuller, the TV host of a popular wedding show, and the next minute the network was shoving five-hundred-thousand-dollars down our throats along with an all-expense-paid wedding and honeymoon. They believed the ceremony of their most eligible bachelor host would give them their highest ratings in the history of their network. I said yes under the circumstances. But now that the day had come, I wasn't so sure I did the right thing.

As my dad and I neared the altar I felt my feet getting heavier and heavier. It was as if I was no longer in control of walking; I had to literally tell myself, right foot, left foot. I was freezing up. My dad must've sensed it because he started to move me along.

"You all right?" he whispered.

"Yes."

He patted my hand and told me, "Relax."

I exhaled and tried to do just that. Upon arriving at the altar, my guests sat. The music winded down to a stop. And the minister began.

"Who giveth this woman away?"

"I do," my father said, gently unlocking our arms. He nodded at Bobby and then took his seat in the front row.

I looked at my groom, a handsome, yellow-toned, muscular man with a smooth baldhead and minimum facial hair. He was a woman's dream, but not mine. And I started to feel extremely bad taking him off the market and possibly keeping him from his true soul mate.

He opened his full and succulent lips to recite his vows and my head started spinning. My heart raced.

My knees were about to buckle. I was on the verge of having a panic attack. I tried to keep it all together but my mind and my body seemed in cahoots on a plan to get me out of the hole I had dug myself into.

My palms sweating, I took several short deep breaths, closed my eyes and opened them again; and suddenly I yelled out "STOP!" in the middle of Bobby saying 'Until death do us part.'

Everybody's eyes swung to me. Bobby's mouth remained opened but the words that were coming from it dissipated.

I looked around and saw a blur of baffled faces, except for Deidre. She was the only one smiling.

"I can't do this!" I proceeded to finish what I had started.

Gasps poured from the attendees.

"What?" Bobby whined, looking at me pitifully.

"I'm sorry," I returned the pity. "It's just that I'm not ready to spend the rest of my life with someone," I said.

More gasps and another pitiful 'What?' from Bobby then I continued, "Especially . . . nnnot a mmman . . ." I stumbled over words. "I'm a lesbian," I confessed.

And before a response or a reaction could be made, I got out of there. But because of my fear of the water, I didn't run like I had planned. Instead, I found myself crawling hastily up the aisle back to shore. It was a beautiful mess.

Sheryl

"I, Sheryl Lee, take you, Eric Andrew Hopkins to be my lawful wedded husband and before God and all these witnesses I promise to be a faithful and true wife in sickness and in health, for richer and for poorer, until death do us part," I repeated, tears breaking free from my eyes.

Eric reached over and gently caught each tear with his thumbs, bringing me in for an early kiss in the process. The love in his eyes was surreal. And as we exchanged quick but passionate kisses, the minister playfully interrupted us. "What's the rush? I'm not getting paid by the hour." Everyone chuckled, including Eric and me. We stepped back in our places and let the minister continue. The whole time staring into each other's eyes anticipating the moment that the minister would pronounce us man and wife.

"If anyone has reason for these two not to wed, speak now or forever hold your peace," the minister said. And right before he started to announce the exchanging of the rings, the doors of the church swung open.

Everybody's attention switched to the back of the church.

"I object!" Kenneth, my ex-husband shouted in a drunken voice. He staggered down the aisle, wearing a wrinkled dress shirt and pants that didn't match, looking horrid.

"Do you know this man?" the minister asked me in amazement.

Meanwhile, Eric's brother and best man quickly walked toward Kenneth.

"Yo, yo, yo," he called out to Kenneth as he held his hand out to stop him from coming any closer.

I was scared and embarrassed, and wished Eric's brother would quickly escort Kenneth out so we could continue our wedding.

"I said, I object!" Kenneth shouted, stopping halfway down the aisle. Then suddenly, Kenneth pulled a handgun from his waistband and aimed it directly at me.

Everything seemed to stand still as I locked my eyes on the barrel. Frightened stiff I can't remember what I said or did at the moment Kenneth stated, "If I can't have you, no one can." Followed by a couple deafening pops.

"AAAAAAARRRRRRRRR!" I screamed in complete terror, just as Eric's heavy frame knocked me to the floor, and out of danger.

I could see people scattering and hear them screaming. The minister and all the groomsmen left the altar and were in the middle of the aisle crowded around Kenneth, apparently beating him and holding him down until the police arrived.

Ramona, and my sister, Liz, scurried over to me, staying low to the floor in case more shots rang out.

"Are you all right, Sheryl?" Ramona asked, fear in her eyes.

"I can't move," I cried. "Eric, Eric, I'm okay. I just need you to let me up," I squealed.

"Eric, let her up." My sister tried assisting me.

"Eric?" Ramona tried lifting Eric's broad shoulder.

"Oh my God." I read my sister's lips.

Then looking up at my husband who was lying on top of me, I noticed he was not breathing. In a panic I started squirming to get from under him and get him some help.

"HELP! HE'S NOT BREATHING! WE NEED TO GET HIM TO A HOSPITAL!"

At that point, Eric's brother, uncle, and several friends left Kenneth in the hands of the other guys and rushed over. They lifted Eric off me slowly and carefully, and it was then that reality struck. Eric had been shot in the chest when he jumped in front of the bullet meant for me.

The sight of the blood pouring from his torso and his big, chiseled stature lying limp, drove me into a fit. I started running up the aisle toward Kenneth in a rage. I wanted to kill him. Better yet, I wanted him to kill me. That would've been the only refuge for me at that time. Dying there with Eric — the man I couldn't see myself living without.

Leslie

earing police sirens approaching, I looked out the cab's back window and saw two cop cars following us closely.

"I'm going to have to pull over," the driver said, almost apologetically.

"Why do you think they're stopping us?" I asked. "Do you have tags on this thing? You don't have any taillights out or anything do you? Is all your paperwork straight?" I drilled him.

"Everything is legit with me. It's you they probably want," he said, pulling the cab to the side of Wilshire Boulevard.

"What do you mean me? What would they want me for?"

"For all that damage you did back there, miss," he whined. "You can't go around breaking people's house and car windows and expect not to pay." He was talking to me like I was a five-year-old.

"Well, that bastard broke my heart and I didn't send any cops after his ass!" I retorted.

"Well, miss, the world doesn't work like that."

I huffed and crossed my arms as I watched two cops approached the cab. One went to the driver's window and the other to the passenger window.

"Hello, officers." The driver was being extra nice.

"Hi. How you doin'?" one cop said, peeping back at me. "Sir, is this your cab?"

"Yes."

"Well we got a call from some neighbors along Faring Road that a cab was seen at the property at 461 where there was some disturbance. Apparently someone vandalized the property pretty badly. And the description they gave actually fits your passenger. I'm going to need you two to step out of the car."

I opened the back door and got out. With much attitude I asked, "What description doesn't fit me in Los Angeles? I'm a white woman with blonde hair, blue eyes, and big boobs!"

"Yeah, but unlike every other woman who fits that profile, you're the one wearing a wedding dress," the cop reminded me.

I looked down at the couture gown and rolled my eyes. I guess it wasn't the smartest thing to commit a crime in a damn wedding dress.

"Okay, so what do I have to do? Pay a fine or something? Take me to my house so I can get my checkbook! Get me off Wilshire Boulevard! I'm already humiliated enough!"

"I'm sorry but we're going to have to take you into custody. From there, it'll be up to a judge if you pay a fine or do jail time."

I shook my head in disagreement as I halfway turned to try to open the cab door. Immediately I felt the hands of the officer tugging at my upper arm.

"Ma'am, you're under arrest."

"WHAT? THIS IS INSANE! CALL MY ATTORNEY! THIS IS ILLEGAL WHAT YOU'RE DOING TO ME RIGHT NOW! THAT MAN HAS MANAGED TO SCREW MY WHOLE LIFE UP AND I'M THE ONE GETTING ARRESTED? THIS IS SOME BULLSHIT! MY ATTORNEY'S GOING TO HAVE YOUR ASS!" I ranted and raved while the young police officer handcuffed me and put me in the back of his squad car.

I was placed in a cell, still in my fifty-thousand-dollar wedding dress; then later I was finger printed, had to take a mug shot and everything. After a long, painful twelve hours and two phone calls, I was released on bond. My attorney who paid the five-hundred-dollar bail had picked me up and explained my options during the ride home. I could try to fight the case and have a trial which meant a lot of inconvenience, money, and a likely guilty verdict that would lead to possible jail time; or I could plead guilty and get some of the charges lessened and others knocked off, pay restitution, and probably attend some sort of counseling or anger management classes. I opted for the latter. I was not about to put myself through lengthy court proceedings knowing got damn well I was guilty as charged.

"Miss DiRosa, you're ordered by the court to pay sixty-two thousand dollars in restitution for the damages you've caused, eighteen hours of one-on-one counseling or twenty-four hours in an anger management program, and you mustn't come within 150 yards of Frank Gastin or his wife Mary Gastin for the next five years.

Boom! The gavel went down and I was standing there before the court frustrated," I told my therapist, Anna Brooks of the prestigious, Brooks and Ledger Psychiatry.

She looked at me with that puzzled face that all psychiatrists seem to wear while their clients are talking to them.

"Why were you frustrated? You got everything you expected, right?" she asked, using her french-manicured fingertips to brush the layered sweep bang from in front of her hazel eyes.

I stood up from the leather chair I couldn't seem to get comfortable in. I walked over to the floor to the ceiling window that gave Anna's office a magnificent view of L.A.'s skyline. "I couldn't understand why there was a restraining order against me! That woman was the one who came to my house and put a gun to my face!"

The puzzled look again as Anna asked, "What woman? And what incident are you referring to?"

I walked away from the window and back to the modern chic, but not so functional, chair. "Do you mind if I smoke a cigarette?" I pulled a pack of Newports from my eighteen-hundred dollar Chanel purse.

"This is a non-smoking facility," she informed me, "but," she stood up in her chair, reached up and untwisted the smoke detector. She removed the batteries from it and left it hanging from its base on the ceiling. "I'll allow it this one time."

"Well I sure appreciate it, Doctor," I lit the cigarette and took a puff. I sat down in the chair and began to tell the doctor my side of the story.

"I was home one evening cooking dinner, finally putting my state of the art chef's kitchen to use. Under my apron I was in nothing more than a Costabella matching bra and panties set and on my feet were a pair of Valentino stilettos. I remember because it was Frank's latest Valentines' gift to me. I had just tasted a pinch of the sea bass I had prepared especially for my date with Frank. It was delicious. I remember thinking to myself; 'You're a bad bitch when you can handle your business in the bedroom *and* in the kitchen.' Just then, my doorbell rang," I set the scene up for Anna as I puffed my cigarette.

"Who said you couldn't turn a hoe into a housewife?" I jokingly asked myself as I pranced to the door. Opening it, I closed my eyes and puckered my lips awaiting a nice juicy kiss from Frank. "You're gonna have to kiss me really good if you want me to open my eyes," I teased.

At that, I felt something press against my lips but it wasn't Frank's soft, warm mouth. It was just the opposite, hard and cold to the touch.

"Frank!" I opened my eyes only to be confronted with a deranged looking black woman holding what looked like Frank's nine millimeter to my mouth. The woman pushed me inside my house and slammed my door behind her.

"Afraid not, sweetheart," she said. "But I am Frank's wife. And it's nice to finally meet you." Her hand was shaking as she kept the gun trained at my face. I was scared to death, tears streaming down my face. "It's not what you think," was the first thing that came to my mind to say.

The woman reached behind her and locked the door. "Oh?" she asked.

"I can explain," I added.

Then the doorbell rang for a second time, and this time I was certain it was Frank. After a brief pause I could hear keys jingling. I opened my mouth to warn him, but . . .

"I wouldn't do that if I were you," Frank's wife said, glaring at me.

She slowly turned around and peeked out the door's window. She snickered, "This nigga come bearing flowers and a gift. Well ain't this about a bitch!"

She moved from in front of the door, guiding my movements with the force of the gun, which now placed against my cheek.

"Get over here and answer the damn door!" she commanded as she took the gun away from my face. "Try to run and I'll shoot both of your sorry asses!" she threatened.

I slowly opened the door. The look of concern covering Frank's face told me he knew something was wrong with me. But instead of him taking my distress as a sign to go get help, he stepped inside the house to console me. As soon as he did, his wife put the gun to his head, forcing him away from the door.

"Mary?" he was shocked.

Instead of responding, she closed and locked the door.

"What the hell are you doing?" he grew argumentative; why I didn't know. I mean, I wasn't the sharpest tool in the shed, but I knew that you don't argue with a person holding a gun to your face.

"I'm joining the party, honey. And you are right on time."

"Doctor, I never been so scared in my life. But did I call the police? No! Did I get restraining orders? No!"

"Well, what did you do?" Dr. Anna asked.

"I listened to Frank talk his wife out of doing anything stupid that would land him dead, her in jail and their two kids parentless. Then after what felt like hours of negotiating they finally left. That's when I packed all my stuff and got out of there. I moved. I needed to be somewhere with twenty-four hour security."

"How did you get back with Frank, then?"

"He called me and begged for my forgiveness. Said he felt soooo bad for putting my life at risk and that he was divorcing his wife once and for all; that her coming to my house yielding a weapon was the final straw. He didn't know what she was capable of and that scared him so he needed to just leave her alone."

"And then what? You took him back?"

"For some stupid ass reason, unbeknownst to me, I believed him -- even though I had heard that story. But that time it was different; it seemed like it anyway. I mean, our lives were in jeopardy and I thought that was the wake-up call Frank needed to follow through with a divorce. I allowed him to come over to my new place, and he dropped down on one knee – with a ring and all – and proposed to me. That's how I knew he was really serious this time. He gave me his Titanium American Express Card the next day, and said I was to start planning the wedding, and to spare no expense. A week after that he gave me the codes to his house and told me to start packing because I would be moving in his mansion with him the minute we returned from our honeymoon."

"And that's what led you to this?"

I nodded my head as I took the last puff on my cigarette. I got up from the chair and walked to the restroom. "I'm gonna flush this," I said of the cigarette butt. "You don't mind, do you?"

"Go ahead," Dr. Anna said. "Well, it looks like our hour is up. But I'm glad you got to set the stage for me. Now, in our next session we can get into some of the issues beneath the surface."

I scratched the back of my hair and asked, "Issues like what, doctor? We can talk about them now because to be honest with you I'm not trying to come back here every week for the next eighteen weeks. I mean, how much do I have to give you to come to an understanding where you and I don't have to see each other for me to make up these hours?"

"I don't take bribes, Ms. DiRosa."

"Well what about over the phone? Can't we do like an hour-long conference call once a week instead of me having to travel down here?"

Dr. Anna shook her head.

I huffed and grabbed my pocketbook. "You're tough, Dr. Anna."

"I'm here to help," she said.

I walked over to the door. She followed me.

"This was a good first session, Ms. DiRosa. I look forward to seeing you next week."

"Yeah, yeah," I sighed. "Have a good one, Dr. Anna."

Angie

I was in the waiting area of my therapist's office collecting all the tabloid and entertainment magazines that had my face plastered on the covers and stuffing them all in my Louis Vuitton Damier Neverfull tote. My plan was to throw them into a dumpster as soon as I left the office. I was in my usual disguise, a black wig styled in a bob, and a pair of dark sunglasses. I didn't want anyone to see me visiting a shrink; I was getting enough bad press for coming out at the altar of my live wedding ceremony – I didn't need to give them anything else to write or talk about.

"Hi, Angie," my doctor said, opening the door to her inner-office. "You can come in." I walked in quickly and was rewarded with a glimpse of her behind as she walked to the chair behind her desk.

For Dr. Anna to be a white woman, she has a nice, round ass, I thought to myself every time.

"So, Angie, how are you today?" she asked, taking her seat.

"I could be better," I admitted.

"Or worse," she pointed out. "Remember that. Whenever you're going through something or are having a tough time, someone somewhere is worse off than you, so be grateful and hopeful."

I took a breath, "I know, I know."

"But do tell me, what's going on?"

I got right to the point. "It's been over a month and they're still talking about it. I still make the cover of some magazines. I mean, why can't they get over it already? It's not like I'm the first person in Hollywood to come out of the closet! I just did it at an awkward time! It's no big deal! It's not like I murdered somebody! That's how they treat me now. Like I killed some damn body. You know I haven't been called for a job since? I was talking to an agent friend of mine and a couple colleagues about it and they all say it's just the temperature of the business right now, but it seems awfully strange to me that just before this incident the temperature was steaming hot. I was being called to direct everything — straight to DVD movies to blockbusters. Now, immediately after the quote, unquote wedding, I can't get a call to direct a damn music video." I gladly dumped my complaints on Dr. Anna.

But before she could say anything, there was a knock on the door.

She looked at me baffled then rose from her chair, but before she could get to the door, it slowly opened a slight crack. Peeping in was a tanned white girl with blonde hair and big titties that turned me on a little.

"I'm sorry, Dr. Anna. I don't mean to bust in on your session like this. I just had a question about this flyer I saw in the folder you gave me," the girl said.

Dr. Anna turned to me, "Do you mind?" she asked.

I shrugged my shoulders and shook my head "Not at all. Go ahead."

"Thanks," the girl said to me with a slight smile. Then she held up a colorful piece of paper with a picture of palm trees, sunshine, and a pretty blue ocean on it. It was the same one I had gotten in the folder Dr. Anna gave me during my first session a couple weeks back.

"I noticed it says that the daily activities that take place during this three-day retreat are equal to five-hour long sessions --"

"Uh huh," Dr. Anna confirmed.

"So does that mean if someone was to go and participate in all the activities for all three days they would accumulate fifteen hours?"

"Correct."

"Okay, now we're talking, Dr. Anna!" the girl said excitedly. "A three-day vacation on this beautiful Tahitian island and I'll walk away with just enough hours to fulfill my court order? Where do I sign up and who do I pay?" The girl whipped a checkbook out of her Chanel bag.

"You can sign up here and pay me. But let's take care of it next week. The money's not due for another two weeks, so you have time," the doctor explained.

"Okay. Well I'll do it next week. Just don't let me forget."

"I won't, Ms. DiRosa."

"Thanks," she turned to walk away. "And I'm sorry again about interrupting your session."

The girl left the office and Dr. Anna closed the door and walked back to her seat, granting me a bonus look at her behind.

"That was for the 'Dress Burning Ceremony'?" I verified.

"Yes. Are you going?"

"I wasn't going to go because the picture reminded me too much of my wedding," I chuckled. Dr. Anna followed suit. "But... if she's going then I might think about it." We shared another little laugh.

"You're so comfortable with your sexuality, so why is it hard for you to face people who are talking about it?" Dr. Anna asked.

Lisa Wu Hartwell
and Miasha

I adjusted my sunglasses pushing them back on the bridge of my nose.

"It's not that it's hard facing them; I don't have a problem with the fact that I came out. It's just that now people are treating me differently. And they're ridiculing me. If they were just saying 'oh look it's Angie Barnes the lesbian' I wouldn't care. But they're saying stuff like 'there's the crazy bitch who ruined Bobby Fuller's life.' And it couldn't be farther from the truth! I didn't ruin his life!"

"That's just speculation," Dr. Anna said. "But why did you go through with the marriage plans in the first place?" she leaned forward resting her chin in the palm of her hand. "I think the combination of having gone through with all the planning and then being live on television at this lavish very expensive wedding ceremony and choosing that to be the time to disclose that pertinent information about yourself is what brings on the ridicule. I mean, had you just said no from the beginning, or anytime before the actual ceremony, things would not have blown up the way they did."

"I understand that, but at the time I was still so confused. And I was just under a lot of pressure. It was like I was caught in a whirlwind of craziness and I couldn't get out."

"Well, here's what I want you to do. I want you to relive that time in your life. And as you're reliving it I want you to point out places where you could've made different choices that would've prevented the outcome that you're living with now. Can you do that?"

I thought about what Dr. Anna was asking of me before nodding my head, "Yeah, I can."

"I think doing that will help you to understand other people's criticism, and thus allow you to come out of hiding. And I believe once you become accountable for where you went wrong and face the world again, your career and your life will get back on track."

I exhaled and sat back in the burnt orange leather chair. I relaxed. I closed my eyes and I just started talking.

I had just left a party in the hills for a group of investors out of Vegas. Feeling good about the possibility of them putting up twenty-five million dollars for a film I was called on to direct, I decided to take the scenic route home. The top was down on my red Porsche as I coasted down the Pacific Coast Highway, meditating to the sounds of Kem. The fresh air felt so good blowing through my locks, and I ran my fingers through them a couple times, feeling proud of who I was and what I had accomplished for myself.

I pulled up to my Mediterranean estate in Sherman Oaks and the sensors on my car granted me automatic entry to the brass and iron gates that I joked were the closest thing to a man that I had in years. They were dark, strong and made me feel secure.

My house resembled a six star hotel lit for the holidays. The numerous palm trees were adorned with clear lights specifically for nights like this one when I returned home alone, which came quite often, might I add.

"All this and no one to share it with," I sighed as I drove into my garage and put my car in park.

I got out the car and instantly felt the need for a massage. It had been a long day from the office to the gym back to the office and then to a party. I wondered if Deidre was in the house. She was my massage therapist and close friend; and one of the few people I trusted with a key to my house. Some nights she would be here waiting for me to get home so she could give me a deep tissue massage before I went to sleep. She said it was good to relieve tension in the muscles before going to bed so you wouldn't wake up with aches and pains and you'd be well rested. The girl sure earned her fifty-thousand-dollars a year salary.

I walked up the stairs of the garage and turned the doorknob and walked into a pitch dark house. I frowned, wondering why all the lights were out. I always left certain lights on, and instructed my staff to do the same. I sensed something was wrong and quickly turned around and headed back to my car, but standing at the foot of the stairs in my garage was a naked Caucasian man. My first thought was to run, and I quickly spun around and darted in my house; but the nude trespasser was at my heels.

"HELP!" I screamed frantically.

"I'm not here to hurt you," he claimed. "You don't remember me? I auditioned for you last week. You said I wasn't believable."

I dug around in my Louboutin clutch for my cell phone. Retrieving it, I dialed 911.

"I'll do anything for this role. Let me audition. Right here. Right now," he continued on, still chasing me through my house.

I stopped in my kitchen, my back against the custom colored dishwasher. I positioned my keys between my fingers creating a weapon. "I need you to leave right now! Get out!" I demanded as stern and as fearless as I could possibly be.

The strange man didn't take heed. He started walking toward me slowly pleading, "You don't understand. This is my last chance. This could be your last chance," he babbled.

I prepared myself to swing at the man and prayed I would get the upper hand. And just as I got into a fighting stance, I saw Deidre appear over the guy's head with one of my very expensive vases from Sierra Leone. I closed my eyes tight to keep from seeing what was to come of my precious, rare vase.

Crack!

I slowly opened my eyes and saw the man on my kitchen floor in a fetal position, holding his bleeding head with both his hands. On top of him and surrounding him, were bits and pieces of one of my most prized possessions. I cringed at the thought of losing such a piece in such a way, but my life was so much more important and so I swiftly wiped the thought out my mind and hugged Deidre for saving it.

"Girl, I need a man, somebody here on a regular basis to deter fools like this!" I said breathlessly.

To that Deidre looked me in my eyes and then planted a long, soft, and passionate kiss on my lips. "Does it have to be a man?" she asked.

"Was that your first lesbian encounter?" Dr. Anna asked.

"Yes," I said. "And it was also the first time I felt a strong need to find a man. I didn't think I was a lesbian at that point, although I liked the kiss. But I just thought I was confused, or that I was just vulnerable because Deidre just saved my life. So, I figured if I got a man then I wouldn't think about Deidre nor the kiss and I could go on and be straight."

"Is that how you came to meet Bobby Fuller?"

I nodded. "I was on the prowl. I put the word out to my close associates that I was looking for somebody. In no time, I was set up on a date with Bobby. We had fun, too. We laughed a lot and clicked really well. We started spending a lot of time together. He would come to my house a lot and I to his. We went to sporting events together, the movies, restaurants, bowling, you name it. We were like best friends overnight. Then for my birthday he invited me out to this real nice restaurant, which he had the chef close down just for us. I went to the bathroom to wash my hands just before our entrees came out and when I got back I knew something was up. Bobby was already on one knee holding an opened box with a sparkling two-carat ruby and diamond ring in it.

How could I have said no to that? And on top of that, as soon as I said yes, all these people appeared out of the woodworks. I was on hidden camera the whole time for his damn TV show. So now, the producers and everybody swooped in and started instantly planning this wedding talking about they would pay for everything and give us some money for our life rights and all this and all that…"

"Why did you say yes?"

"Because I thought the 'yes' was between me and him. And I figured that some time a little later down the line I would get him alone and tell him that I wasn't ready to settle down just yet. I didn't want to do that in front of the chef and waitress especially after how extravagant and romantic he had set the whole proposal up. But when I found out I was being watched by a whole production crew I felt stuck to my word."

"Meanwhile, what became of you and Deidre?"

"We grew closer. She was the only person I could talk openly to about my confusion; whether I wanted to be with men or women."

"When did it become clear to you that being with women was your choice?"

"The night before the wedding. Deidre was giving me a massage at the beach house the wedding party was staying in. It started to get intimate. The next thing I knew we were having sex for the first time. I knew then that I was indeed a lesbian."

"So that's why it took you up until the wedding day to call it off? You weren't sure until then?"

"Basically," I huffed. "I was just trying to go all the way with the wedding thing hoping I would start to feel it at some point."

"Well, in reality, you did the right thing, Angie. Even though you waited to the last minute, you did fess up. Many people would've continued on, exchanged vows, and became husband and wife and just carried on an adulterous affair during the marriage, wasting their spouse's time and life and ultimately hurting everybody involved. But you didn't do that. You actually put yourself, your career, and your reputation on the line to keep Bobby Fuller from wasting his time and his life. You should be thanked." Dr. Anna finally saw it my way.

"I agree, Dr. Anna," I said. "But how do we get the world to feel the same way we do."

"You have to face them. You have to get rid of the disguise. You have to stop scouting out all magazines with your story in them, and you have to confront rumors, speculations, and exaggerations with the truth."

"Howwww?" I whined.

Dr. Anna summed it up with one final suggestion, "Come on the trip. I think it'll do you a lot of good."

**Lisa Wu Hartwell
and Miasha**

Sheryl

I was driving on the freeway headed downtown to an appointment with my psychiatrist. I must've been driving too slowly because I noticed people going around me and giving me nasty looks as they passed me. I started hearing horns blowing and I looked in my rearview mirror. The car behind me was riding my tail. *Let me get out this lane and let him pass,* I said to myself. Then I just burst into tears. I was having another breakdown.

I needed to get off the freeway and gather my composure. I put my right blinker on and inched across the four lanes to the exit lane, got off and drove to a nearby gas station where I parked my car and leaned my head on the steering wheel. I just cried.

After a few minutes, the tears dried up and I felt capable of getting back on the road. It was becoming a reoccurring incident. I would be driving somewhere and have to pull over to cry. My emotions were so out of whack and uncontrollable I feared they were beginning to take over my life.

That is why I even agreed to counseling. My best friend, Ramona bugged me about it nearly everyday after I witnessed my ex-husband murder my fiancé. She was convinced I was depressed and sure enough she was right. I was diagnosed three weeks ago. I'd been put on anti-depressants and made to see my psychiatrist twice a week. But even still I have my moments where I just feel overly sad and unenthused about life. I keep waiting for something miraculous to happen to get me out of this slump and sometimes I wonder if it's going to take another thirteen years for that to happen. And just the thought of having to wait that long for freedom again sends me right back in depression mode.

Thanks to my unstable emotions and inability to focus while driving, I arrived at my appointment twenty-minutes late again. Nevertheless, Dr. Anna greeted me with a smile and patience.

"Another episode?" she asked after I had taken a seat in her office.

I nodded, somewhat ashamed and embarrassed.

Dr. Anna looked at me, seemingly studying me. I didn't return the eye contact. Instead I kept my head low. I just wanted her to pass the hour away with suggestions of what I could do to get better like she normally did so I could go.

Dr. Anna had other plans. I glanced up after sitting in awkward silence for at least ten minutes.

"Why aren't you saying anything, Doctor?"

"Well, because I want you to do the talking today, Sheryl. This is your sixth session with me. And you have yet to open up. I think your emotions can be much more manageable if you'd release some of what you're bottling up inside you."

I wasn't ready to talk. But, because I was tired of crying and sleeping through life, I felt like I should give it a try. Something had to give and if it was a must that it be me then I would.

"What do you want to know, Dr. Anna?" I exhaled.

"I wanna know what gave you the courage and the strength to leave your husband of thirteen years?"

I hesitated as I played in my head the events that led up to me finally walking out on Kenneth almost two years ago. I let out a sigh and then began to tell my story.

It was a cool spring afternoon. I had parked my pearl white Cadillac Escalade beside Kenneth's silver Hummer in our driveway. I squinted my eyes trying to see through the almost-illegal tinted windows to see if Kenneth was inside his truck. He wasn't. Thank God, I thought. That meant I had a few more minutes of peace.

I reached down to get my cell phone which had fallen to the floor while I was driving.

"Three missed calls?" I mumbled. "That's all I need."

I grabbed my off-white Hermes Birkin bag out the passenger seat and tossed my phone inside it. I opened my car door and stepped out. Throwing my bag over my shoulder, I pulled down on my baseball cap as if I was getting ready to play ball.

"Here we go," I said under my breath.

I walked toward the enormous front doors of my eight-bedroom estate, sizing it up as I went.

"It is absolutely breathtaking, he's right. Any woman would love to be in my shoes," I thought as I took in the beauty of the Japanese gardens, the waterfalls, the exotic fish that cost more than some people's mortgage and the handpicked statues flown in from Italy. It was certainly a palace fit for a queen.

I got inside and hiked up the winding marble staircase, then walked to the master suite and grabbed for the door. Taking a deep breath I opened it. Kenneth was there to greet me as he had been often lately. Having recently stepped down from his executive position at Karma Films, he had too much time on his hands. And whenever he was home he expected me to be there, too. He looked at his watch then at me, up and down.

"I called you. Where have you been?" he asked as I walked past him toward the bathroom.

"I called you right back and you didn't answer," I told him.

"Then I called you again. Still no answer."

"I didn't realize my phone was on vibrate," I called out to him as I came out of my cashmere Juicy Couture warm up. "Then it fell on the floor while I was driving," I added, turning on the rain shower system.

"What were you doing?" Kenneth appeared in the doorway of our bathroom.

I was down to my bra and panties and the way he was looking at me frightened me. I wished I hadn't opted to take a shower right away. Because me doing so gave him just the ammunition he needed to go off on me.

"You were out fuckin' some other nigga, weren't you?" he fumed, coming closer to me. "Fuck you takin' a shower for?" He pinned me against my vanity and jammed his hand in my panties.

I stood stiff as he shoved each of his fingers inside me. Taking them out, he smelled them, and then with an evil smirk he licked each of them one by one.

"You're sick you know that!" I was disgusted, and struggled to break loose. But Kenneth gripped me by my arms, forcing me to the floor.

"You were born a hoe and you'll die a hoe," he stood over me, unbuckling his belt and pulling his pants down.

Tears invaded my eyes and marched down my face like an army. Wordless and spineless, I lie there crying, adding more pain and misery to my collection.

I started to cry as I told Dr. Anna the story; the pain it brought up was unbearable. It was one of the worst days of my life, and going through it again was difficult.

"It's okay to cry, Sheryl." Dr. Anna's voice offered little comfort. "Just work through the tears. Keep talking. Push past the pain. Don't stop when it gets tough or you'll always find yourself defeated."

I wiped my eyes, took a deep breath, and decided to take Dr. Anna's advice. I kept talking.

"He raped me, sodomized me, then he beat me. But what's crazy is that I endured all of that and still hadn't worked up the nerve to leave that man. It wasn't until he lashed out at me verbally that I felt it was time for me to go . . ."

Kenneth finished scrubbing my blood off his hands and walked back into our bedroom where I had managed to drag myself to after the abuse. I lay in the bed -- in just my bra -- weak, physically in pain, and bleeding from my nose and my rectum. I was sobbing to the point that I had lost my voice. Yet for some reason he didn't feel he had hurt me enough.

"You know what I can't understand?" he asked, not expecting an answer. "I can't understand why I worry about who you giving your pussy to? I mean, no man in his right mind wants that worn out shit. The only reason I put up with it is 'cause it's convenient. But every chance I get, I'm looking for fresh pussy, you can believe that," he scoffed.

The words felt like daggers piercing my heart and soul. There I was lying there battered and bruised, defenseless, and he had the audacity to tell me that he was actively cheating on me every chance he got.

Suddenly out of nowhere I got a burst of energy. I jumped up out the bed and I screamed with what little voice I had left, "I HATE YOU KENNETH! YOU ARE ONE SHIT-POOR EXCUSE FOR A MAN! I'M LEAVING YOU! AND THE NEXT TIME I SEE YOU I HOPE IT'S IN YOUR CASKET!"

Kenneth did nothing but laugh sadistically. I stomped over to my closet, threw on some clothes, then went in the bathroom and washed my face. Left the bedroom, jogged down the stairs, and walked out the door. Kenneth didn't try to stop me either. I guessed he figured I would go cool off and come right back like I had done every other time. But I didn't. I drove across town to Ramona's two-bedroom loft and I didn't look back.

Leslie

"Oh, yes, that's stunning!" I picked up a Jean Paul Gaultier cutout one-piece swimsuit. "I can definitely see me wearing this on a Tahitian beach, sucking down a pink Mai Tai, admiring the native surfers."

"Yeah, I can see that," my younger sister Renee agreed.

"Okay, I need this in a size six." I scoured through the rack. "Where are the workers in this place? I have a dozen items in my hand, you would think someone would've offered to start me a dressing room by now!"

"Why are you so angry all the time?" Renee asked.

"I'm not! I'm only angry when people make me angry! It's not like I wake up this way!"

"You sure about that?"

"Screw you, Renee." I walked away from the rack of swimwear and over to a nearby cash register. The woman ringing up a customer's clothes peeped up at me.

"Can I help you?" she asked.

"Um, take a guess. I have a shit-load of clothes draped over my arm and no one has started me a dressing room yet! Where's your manager?" I snapped.

"Oh my God," my sister said under her breath while subtly distancing herself from me.

I waited impatiently at the register while the cashier called her manager. Minutes later a short stubby redhead approached me.

"Is there a problem?" she asked me.

"I just want some customer service around here, that's all. I would like to continue shopping but my arm is about to fall off lugging all these clothes around."

"I'm sorry about that. We're understaffed today, but I'll be happy to put these things in a fitting room for you while you shop." She held out her short arms to collect my items.

I dumped the things and walked away.

"Would you like anything cold to drink while you look around?" She was pouring it on thick.

"Yes, a glass of champagne will do." I made my way back over to the swimsuits.

My sister was already there, holding my size in the Jean Paul Gaultier I was admiring before I was interrupted by the lack of customer service.

"Thank you," I said, taking the bathing suit out of her hand.

"Wouldn't want you to kill anybody," Renee said, mockingly. "I don't wanna have to visit both my siblings in jail."

"Not like you visit one."

"I do visit Danny," she defended.

I stopped shuffling through the racks and stared daggers at my sister.

"Well," she corrected herself, "I *have* visited him."

"Yeah, once."

"I don't know how you do it," she said. "It's so invading and time consuming," she whined at the experience of visiting our brother in prison.

"It's our brother, Renee. We should be willing to jump through hoops of fire to see him."

Renee didn't say anything. She just shrugged her shoulders and made a 'that's true' face and continued browsing.

Lisa Wu Hartwell
and Miasha

I tried on seventeen pieces, and ended up taking all but two to the register. That was what I called a good shopping day. As the cashier rang me up and the amount on the small screen climbed past two thousand dollars, my sister's curiosity was piqued.

"How are you gonna pay for all this?" she asked, wide-eyed.

"With Frank's American Express," I said, as if she should have known.

"What are you still doing with that man's credit card?"

"I can't give it back to him, so…"

"Why can't you?"

"I can't go within a hundred and fifty yards of him, remember?" I snickered.

"Your total is three thousand four hundred sixty-two dollars and sixteen cents," the cashier announced.

I whipped the all black credit card out of my wallet and handed it over nonchalantly.

"You are crazy." My sister shook her head.

I pulled the Dolce and Gabbana shades that were atop my head down over my eyes and said, "Only when you fuck with me." I set the record straight.

Retrieving Frank's card and taking my bags and receipt, I headed out of Saks with my nose in the air. *You wanna be an ass, Frank Gastin, you get wiped,* I amusingly said to myself as I strutted to my Gran Turismo.

Angie

"So you're going?" Deidre asked as she watched me sift through sexy bra and panty sets in the lingerie department of Neiman's.

"Yeah, I'm going to give it a try." I pretended not to be enthused.

Without taking her eyes off my select pieces, she went on to give me her opinions about why I shouldn't go to my therapist's annual 'Dress Burning Ceremony' in Tahiti.

"I don't see what it'll do for you, Angie." She shook her head at one of the bras I held up for her approval. "I mean, it's not like *you* were stood up at the altar. *He* was. If anything he should be recommended to go. Like, what are you possibly going to get out of being on a tropical island for three days surrounded by a bunch of scorned and drunk women?"

I tried to hide my smile as I visualized the picture she painted. I wanted to tell her that was exactly why I was going, but I knew that was exactly what she didn't want to hear. I knew like she knew it was the sole reason she didn't want me to go; she was jealous. I didn't blame her, though. Had I been in her shoes, and felt about her the way she made it clear that she felt about me, I would be jealous, too. But, the fact of the matter was, I wasn't in her shoes and I didn't feel the way she did.

I mean, don't get me wrong, I liked Deidre a lot. And she was very attractive so it was hard not to. Her light brown eyes that sparkled in the sun, shoulder-length copper-colored hair, big dimpled smile and shapely body were all pieces of a perfect puzzle. However, I was just getting familiar with my sexuality and didn't want to restrict it right away. I wanted to explore the side of me that I kept tamed all of my life.

"Well, for me, Dr. Anna said it wasn't about getting over a man or a relationship but about getting over media scrutiny and all the backlash."

Deidre twisted her lips and finally looked up at me. "So, what are you going to burn while everybody else is burning their wedding gowns?"

I shrugged my shoulders. "I guess the collection of magazines and tabloids that tarnished my name in the business."

"Walk me in the dressing room to try this on, please." Deidre abruptly changed the subject.

I dragged my feet as I followed Deidre over to the fitting rooms. I knew what she was up to and it surely wasn't trying on the bustier she had randomly picked up.

An overly made up middle-aged white woman with dirty-blonde hair and gray eyes unlocked a fitting room for us. She gave a polite smile as we went inside and told us to let her know if we needed anything in another size.

As soon as she disappeared, Deidre closed and locked the door. She turned to me, a devilish grin on her face; she gently shoved me until my back was pressed against the wall. I resisted, but only a little. I could never fully turn down sex from Deidre. I admit, I was a sucker for the things that woman could do with her tongue.

She unbuttoned my cutoff jean shorts and slid them down just past my thighs. She positioned herself on her knees as she playfully removed my panties with her teeth. Trying to keep her giggles muted, I reached down and put my hand over her mouth. She removed my hand and got serious, using her mouth to pleasure me in ways no man had ever. I leaned my head back and closed my eyes as I enjoyed Deidre's latest tactic to get me to change my mind about going to Tahiti.

Lisa Wu Hartwell
and Miasha

Sheryl

I was pulling up in front of Bloomingdales at the Beverly Center where Ramona worked as a buyer for their children's department. And, unlike every other Tuesday and Thursday evening I met Ramona there after my therapy session, she stood outside waiting for me.

"I'm sorry, I'm late," I said immediately upon her approaching the passenger door.

"I was starting to get worried," she said, climbing up into my SUV.

"I know. I should have called."

"A crying spell?" she quizzed.

I shook my head.

"Traffic?"

"No. Actually," I cracked a smile, "you're goin' to be proud of me."

"What did you do?"

I glanced over at Ramona. "I opened up in my session today," I revealed proudly.

"Really?" Ramona sang.

"That's why I'm a little late. We ran over the time and everything," I explained.

"Oh, well hell, girl, you should've called me and told me. We could've rescheduled this dinner."

"No, no. It wasn't like we had more to talk about. I poured my whole soul out to the woman; there was nothing left to say."

"Well, how do you feel? Any better?" I could sense Ramona looking at me.

I glanced over at her. "A lot better. I'm not even goin' lie." I then turned my attention back on the road as I drove to The Ivy for our nine o'clock late dinner reservation.

Ramona started clapping joyfully. "I told you!" She took full credit. "Didn't I say it would feel a lot better once you released some of that crap?"

I nodded. "You were right. I don't have a problem admitting that."

"So, now do you think you're going to be more receptive to Dr. Anna's advice?"

"Yeah, I mean, she is the expert. I guess I need to let her do the job I'm paying her to do."

"Exxx-actly," Ramona emphasized.

It got silent for about a minute, then Ramona asked, "So, are you going to go on that trip she told you about?"

A quick glance over at Ramona then back to the traffic that was coming to a slow stop ahead of me, "I don't know about all that."

"All what? A therapeutic vacation? What's there not to know?"

"It's not that I wouldn't want to go --"

"Then what's stopping you, Sheryl? I think it could be so refreshing and much needed."

"I do, too," I agreed, picturing myself lying out on a peaceful beach, taking in the fresh air, bathing in the sun. "It's just that, I don't wanna keep digging in my savings. At least not until after the spousal support hearing. I don't know what all I'll get if anything. Kenneth got all these powerful lawyers trying to use the fact that when I got with Eric that he figured he was off the hook. You never know how this is all goin' to play out. I'm just tryin' to maintain right now. I don't have it to be doin' much more."

"I understand," she said. "Although I'm sure once your lawyers explain that Kenneth murdered Eric, who was your only means of support, you'll get everything you need." She gazed out the window. "But it doesn't hurt to spend more wisely these days. I feel that."

A brief silence again. Then Ramona broke it, "But me on the other hand, I don't have a spousal support hearing pending and I have rights to my stash whenever and for whatever I want it so..."

I shot Ramona a look. "So what?!"

"I wanna pay for your trip for you," she said.

"Ahn ahn . . .Nope . . . Not a chance," I protested. "I cannot let you do that. I appreciate it, but I can't."

"Girl, please. You know the last time I heard somebody say the words *let* and *you* in the same sentence? That's why I ain't never been married as it is. I'm single and independent for a reason. That reason being so that I can do whatever the hell I want to with each and every aspect of my life. And right now, I *want* to pay for your Tahiti trip," Ramona ran it down. "It's my wedding gift to you," she added.

My eyebrows furrowed. "Ramona, you already got me a wedding gift."

"Yeah, but unfortunately you never got to enjoy it. So, I'm asking you to take this new gift from me. And enjoy it."

I no longer argued against Ramona's gesture. And it was not because I had given in to her. It was just that, I found it overwhelmingly nice of Ramona to offer such a gift and my getting emotional over having a true friend like her along with my contemplating whether or not I was going to accept her offer kept me quiet for the rest of the drive to Robertson Boulevard. Silently, though, I thanked her — and for far more than the Tahiti trip.

Leslie

I eagerly jumped out of the limousine at LAX. It was going to be scorching hot in L.A., you could tell. It was only ten a.m. and the humidity was already thick. I pulled my Gucci sunglasses down over my eyes while waiting for the driver to remove my three-piece Louis Vuitton luggage from his trunk.

Meanwhile I waved for a skycap to come begin the process of checking me in.

"Good morning maam," a young Latino responded to my call.

"Yes, it sure is," I told him. "But do you know what would make it all the better?"

He smirked and shook his head, "No, what would that be?"

"If you could get me checked in without me having to wait in that line." My eyes locked on the line of passengers stretching from Delta's curbside check-in booth.

The young guy smirked again. I pulled out a fifty-dollar bill and flashed it before his impressionable eyes. He nonverbally agreed to my request as he gathered my suitcases onto a luggage cart and started walking them over to be weighed.

"Have a good trip," the driver said, after closing the car trunk.

"Thanks," I replied, trying to keep my eye on my luggage while peeling a hundred dollar bill from the wad of cash I had gotten from the bank, thanks to

Frank's American Express. "Here you are," I called out to the older gentlemen.

He walked back over to me and reached his hand out to accept his tip. "Thank you, ma'am," he said, gratefully.

I then met up with the skycap weighing my last piece of luggage. He informed me that my first bag was over the weight limit and would require an additional fifty dollars fee. I paid the fine no problem. I then gave him his money for expediting my check-in. Another skycap who was behind the booth motioned for my ID. I gave it to him.

"Where are you headed to?" he asked.

"Tahiti," I said, joyfully. "Aloha."

"Aloha," he chuckled. "That's Hawaiian."

"You say tomatoe, I say tomato," I flagged him.

He smiled. "Here's your boarding pass, Ms. Leslie DiRosa. You're at Gate C."

"Thank you." I took the documents, saw my luggage onto the conveyor belt, and headed to my gate.

At the security checkpoint, there was yet another long line and I asked myself, *Who plans a trip in late August when everybody and their mothers are going on vacation?*

Thank God I was a first-class passenger; otherwise, I would have had to scope out an opportunity to get to the front of the line. But in my case, I was able to get in a shorter line — a much shorter line, reserved specifically for those flying first-class.

I practically got undressed before walking through the metal detectors and handing the security attendant my boarding pass. After he returned it I got my belongings out of the buckets, reassembled myself and was off to my gate.

On the way, I stopped at a bookstore and skimmed through about a dozen fashion and travel magazines until I found four I wanted. I also purchased some Altoids since I planned to drink multiple glasses of vodka on the plane and a bottled water for the half of Ambien I planned to take right before getting on.

I swiped Frank's trusty ol' credit card and took my items. From there it was to Brookstone, a store that sold electronics and comfort products like neck pillows and massagers. I figured I'd rack up on things that would keep me occupied and comfy for the eight-hour flight I had ahead of me. After looking at all the gadgets and trying them out twice I bought a Sony Reader so that I could download and read e-Books, some noise canceling headphones in case I was stuck with a crying baby on board, a heated gel neck pillow to replace the flimsy pillow they give you on the plane, and a pair of the softest slippers I had ever felt in my life just for the hell of it. *Swipe*. I was beginning to think having Frank's card was more fun than having Frank.

By the time I got to my gate I was in need of another suitcase. It was as if I went Christmas shopping in the airport. I had time to eat my fruit salad, take half my sleeping pill and finish my water before I was called to board. I got on the plane, put my shopping bags in the overhead bin and took my window seat in the second row.

I swapped my Chanel peep-toe pumps for the cozy slippers I had just purchased and sunk into the plush leather seats. Starting with the latest issue of Vanity Fair, I decided to read as many of my magazines as I could before the Ambien kicked in.

In between skimming the pages of my magazines I would glance up to check out each passenger boarding the plane after me. I admit it's prejudiced, but I tended to scope out the Arab passengers more so than everybody else. I thought if I looked at them long enough I could sense whether or not they were up to something. And so far, so good.

My eye got drawn to an article in *Us Weekly* about the director chick in Hollywood who stood up 'Million Dollar Marriage' host, Bobby Fuller. I remembered hearing the story a little while back when it first broke and it stuck with me since the wedding disaster took place on the same date as my own. I never did get the full story, though, so I thought it'd be a good read. I was about a third down the page when a soft-spoken woman saying, "Excuse me", interrupted me.

I looked up to see this gorgeous Asian and Black-looking chick waiting to take the seat beside me. She had glowing light-brown skin and straight black hair that flowed down her back. Her features were amazing—high cheek bones, slanted eyes, and perfectly full lips. The type of face women like me would pay for. I almost couldn't stop staring at her.

"I'm sorry," she said, as she stood in the aisle waiting for me to move the rest of my magazines and headphones off her seat.

"Oh, no, I'm sorry," I said, moving my things. "I didn't realize this was a full flight."

"Thank you," she said, making herself comfortable.

Right away I called for a flight attendant.

"Hi, yes, do you have a first class seat available I can purchase?" I asked the chipper, blonde curly-headed stewardess.

Leaning in, she asked, "You mean you want to change to another first class seat?" she asked, blinking her sky-blue eyes.

"No. I'm fine where I am. I just need some more room for all my things," I explained.

She paused as if I were speaking a foreign language, then acted as if she needed further clarification. "I don't understand. You want to buy a second seat, in addition to the one you're sitting in, simply to hold your things? What things, ma'am?"

I held up my magazines.

"You know you can put them in the overhead bins or in a pocketbook under the seat in front of you."

"Yeah, but if I put them in a bin, I won't be able to access them as frequently as I would like. And who's gonna feel like bending down every two seconds to get something from under the seat in front of me?"

"Well how about the seatback pocket in front of you?"

"Germs," I twisted my lips and turned up my nose.

"Well, unfortunately you cannot put your items in a seat. They have to be securely stowed during the flight," she was less polite.

"Fine," I gave up trying to buy an additional seat. Yes, I was deliberately trying to break Frank's bank, but I wasn't going to fight trying to do it. Besides, there would be plenty of opportunities to spend his money in Tahiti anyway.

As the stewardess walked toward the cockpit, a final passenger barged on the plane, out of breath and somewhat disheveled. She looked up at the letters above the seats and down at her crinkled up boarding pass, then she sat in one of the two seats across the aisle from where the beauty queen and I were sitting.

I watched her only to see if it appeared she had a guest joining her and when it seemed she'd be sitting without someone right next to her, I decided to ask if I could put my things in the vacant seat.

"Excuse me." I reached over the pretty woman. She assisted me by getting the last-minute lady's attention.

"Yes?" the lady asked as she turned to look in our direction.

Immediately what I was going to ask her went out the window and what was more important was the fact that I knew this lady.

"I know you!" I blurted.

Her eyes lit up and she said, "From Dr. Anna's office right?"

I frowned and shook my head. "No. I know you from this 'Million Dollar Mistake' article!" I held up the magazine open to the page I was reading. I excitedly smiled from ear-to-ear, because the woman I just read about in the magazine was sitting right across from me on the plane. Not that I was star-struck or anything -- living in Los Angeles you run into stars all the time - it was just that it was extremely coincidental. A sign even. For what, I didn't know, but I was excited, nonetheless.

Too bad she didn't share my excitement. Instead she rolled her eyes. "That is soooo old," she sighed.

Meanwhile the girl next to me butted in.

"I'm sorry. I don't mean to be rude. But I heard you say you thought you knew her from Dr. Anna's office," she said to the obviously embarrassed director.

She nodded. "Despite where she recognizes me from, I recognize her from there."

"Well, I do go to a Dr. Anna in Beverly Hills," I said, trying to redeem myself.

"I do, too," the girl next to me said.

"We all must be headed to the Dress Burning Ceremony," I concluded.

The pretty girl cracked a half smile and nodded and the embarrassed girl said, "Yeah, I knew you were going." She pointed to me. "You were eager to pay the minute you found out you could be done with therapy after the three days on this trip."

"Ohhhhh," I suddenly recalled the incident. "You were the one whose session I busted in on…"

"Riiight," she sang. "That's where I thought you were going to say you knew me from."

"Well, I don't remember you having dreadlocks."

"They're called locks," she corrected me, "And you know what? You're right. I had on a wig that day."

"See, so how could I have remembered you from there?"

"True," she said. "In your defense, I *was* in disguise."

"Well anyway, I'm Leslie," I held out my hand.

"Angie," she said, giving me a firmer handshake than I anticipated. "And you are?" She looked to the girl next to me.

"Sheryl," she smiled and shook Angie's hand.

"Sheryl? You don't look like a Sheryl," I gave my two cents.

"I know, right," Angie agreed. "You look too exotic to be named Sheryl."

"Don't she?" I nodded to Angie. Then turning to Sheryl I suggested, "Your name should be something like Jade, Destiny or Diamond, or something…"

Sheryl chuckled.

Angie wrinkled her face and said, "Those are stripper names!"

"But you know what I'm saying," I argued.

"Yeah . . . but I'm thinking more like . . ." she stared at Sheryl.

Sitting upright in her seat, Sheryl was looking at Angie and me like we were crazy as we went back and forth about her name.

"Alize or Tila Tequila," Angie completed her thought.

"She looks like she was born on an island not in a state store!" I contended.

Sheryl started laughing, as did Angie and myself. It was as if the three of us had known one another all our lives and were taking a trip together. None of us knew that what would come of that meeting would be something strong and long lasting, yet fragile and almost too short.

It was a gift and a curse meeting Angie and Sheryl — two women who would impact my life forever.

Lisa Wu Hartwell
and Miasha

Sheryl

Iarrived at the Motu Mute airport in Bora Bora ready to get in a town car and be taken to my oceanfront suite where I could stretch out in the king sized bed and get a comfortable nap. But waiting to transport me to the hotel was no car, but a boat. So instead of slipping my feet out of my Gucci flip-flops and gliding them across the cozy carpet of a backseat, champagne in hand, I was toting my luggage onto a Ferry with hard, wooden floors and seats to match.

No complaints, though. The weather was warm but not stuffy and the tranquil blue sea was mesmerizing. Already I could see just how much I needed this vacation.

And I wasn't the only one. The boat ride to our resort, all my newfound friends, Angie, a chic, afro-centric type and Leslie, an over-the-top material girl talked about was how bad they needed a get-away.

Twenty or so minutes later and we docked at the St. Regis resort. Paradise, if I had to describe the resort in one word. Once off the boat, Angie, Leslie and I walked to the front desk together. We took our places in the lengthy line of mostly women who appeared to be between the ages of twenty-five and forty-five. I looked at each of them, head to toe. Some looked extremely happy, some unenthused, others excited and a few timid. And suddenly a strong sense of sadness overcame me. I wondered if being surrounded by so many women was a glimpse into my future. Would I be forever single and lonely? My life spent on all-girl vacations, shopping excursions, and weekend casino trips? I hoped not. Not that there was anything wrong with any of those activities. It was just that I wasn't that type. I was more of a relationship girl. I loved the company of a man, romance, and having a family. And to imagine myself going the rest of my life without those was overwhelmingly depressing. For a second I felt like I was going to have an episode and break out into a crying spell. But luckily for me, I was next up to check-in.

"Good day. Welcome to St. Regis. Are we checking in today?" the average-height, brown-skinned, dark, shiny haired guy asked.

"Yes," I smiled.

"Can I have your name?"

"Sheryl Lee."

The guy typed something, I guessed my name, into his computer and watched the screen. After a few seconds, he said, "Thank you Ms. Lee. So you're here for the Annual Dress Burning Ceremony?"

I forced a grin and nodded, wondering why the reason I was there wasn't anonymous.

"You're in for a good time, then," he assured. "Can I have a major credit card and your driver's license please?" he requested, his eyes glued to the computer monitor in front of him.

I handed the guy what he had asked for and waited while he made a copy of my license and swiped my card. He punched some more data into his computer and then handed me my keys and a brochure detailing the activities Dr. Anna had planned for her group.

Leslie

"You've got to be kidding me! What?"

The short, caramel-complexioned, native looked at me sorrowfully and repeated, "Your card has been declined."

Shaking my head in disbelief, I advised, "Try it again. There must be a mistake."

She swiped the card.

"That is a black card," I announced. "Do you know what a black card is?"

She nodded slowly as we both waited for the machine to read a response.

"It's a credit card that has no limit on it. You understand that? So it is impossible for it to be declined. It's an indeclinable card!" I snapped.

The lady nodded again as she handed me the card. "It's not working, ma'am."

I snatched the card and jammed it in my wallet. "That son of a bitch," I mumbled, picturing Frank's face in my mind. "He done cut me off," I concluded.

"Would you like to put a different credit card on file?"

"Of course. That's the only way I'm going to be accommodated isn't it?" I pulled a Platinum Visa from my wallet and reluctantly handed it over to the clerk. I took a deep breath as she swiped it. It was my debit card. And if it were declined then I would have a serious problem. That would mean Frank wiped me out and I was dead broke besides the five hundred dollars in cash I had on me. I felt beads of sweat gather at my temples as I waited.

The woman looked at the machine then back up at me. A slow nod and she confirmed my worst fear. "Insufficient funds, ma'am."

I wanted to jump over the counter and ring the clerk's neck but it wasn't her fault my bastard ex-fiancé had screwed me once again. Trying my hardest to maintain my composure, I took the card back and placed it in my wallet.

"Okay . . ." I huffed. "Let me downgrade from the over-water bungalow to a regular suite please," I requested, calmly.

The woman punched some keys on her computer's keypad. Then she bared more bad news. "I'm sorry ma'am, we are all sold out of the regular suites."

I felt like I was having a fucking nightmare. "Well, what do you have that's cheaper than the bungalow?"

"Nothing available for this weekend. We are all booked up."

"So then what the fuck am I supposed to do?" I could no longer compose myself.

"Either pay for the bungalow that you reserved or you may have to consider another resort."

"THIS IS SOME BULLSHIT!" I lost it. "GET YOUR MANAGER OUT HERE, RIGHT NOW!"

At that outburst, everybody's eyes traveled in my direction. And out the corner of mine I saw the two women I met on the plane cautiously approaching me.

"What's the problem?" Angie asked, a look of concern sprawled across her face.

"That bastard took all my money out my account, cut my access to his credit card, and they're sold out of regular suites!"

A taller woman appeared behind the counter next to the clerk who had been trying to get me checked in.

"Ma'am, I understand you want to cancel your reservation and downgrade. Is that correct?"

"Yes!"

"Well, that would be fine if we had vacancies available. The best we can do is put you in a bungalow until Sunday afternoon."

"How is that supposed to help me?!"

"Leslie," Sheryl took my attention away from the helpless manager. "Why don't you just stay with me in my room? I have double beds. I don't mind," she kindly offered.

Angie's eyes lit up as I contemplated taking Sheryl up on her offer. They both seemed to think it was a good idea but I was a little hesitant. I mean, it was nice of her, don't get me wrong. But I just met her. I didn't know what her living habits were. And to be cooped up in a 600 square foot hotel room with her for three days could turn out to be a disaster. I didn't know about that.

"You know what?" Angie sparkled, "How 'bout me and Sheryl cancel our rooms and the three of us go in on the bungalow you reserved?"

I glanced at Sheryl. She shrugged. I looked at the hotel manager and the front desk clerk. They both smiled, the manager nodding.

"That could work," I approved. Shit, did I really have a choice? And besides I'd rather share a whole bungalow than one tiny room.

"Okay ladies, let me get you all taken care of," the clerk said, happily.

We checked into our over-water bungalow, and it was every bit amazing. If only I could have had it to myself. That damn Frank, I thought. I wished I could have one more night with him. And not for sex either. What I'd give to be in the presence of that man while he slept.

After running through the bungalow like we were cast members on a reality show touring our temporary digs, my roommates and I went our separate ways. The two of them to unpack. Me, to take a nap. According to the brochure I was given at check-in, there was a meet-and-greet dinner later on. So I'd better get my rest now. I closed the door to my room, which I didn't have to share, thank God. Put my luggage against the wall. Lay down on the white, fluffy, bedding and closed my eyes. It had been a long day.

Angie

"Oh my God, Deidre, I didn't know it was a room in the middle of the damn ocean!" I whispered into the phone. I was sitting on the toilet seat, elbows resting on my knees while seeking comfort from my friend with benefits. "You can literally feed fish from under the coffee table!"

"I told you you shouldn't have gone," Deidre spited.

"I didn't reserve an over-the-water bungalow. I reserved a regular ocean-view room," I explained.

"Then why are you staying in a bungalow then?"

"This girl I met on the plane…"

"Oh here we go!" Deidre cut me off. "Don't tell me you're going to be spending the weekend in an over-water suite with some chick you just met on the plane! That's some real hoe shit, Angie! You waste no time, huh? Is that why you wanted to go so bad? So you could lap it up with some vulnerable freak bitches in luxurious accommodations?"

"Ho, ho, hold on a minute! It's nothing like that," I attempted to correct her. "She didn't have the money to pay for her room and there weren't any more cheaper rooms available. So me and this other girl I met on the plane, the three of us go to the same doctor —- we both canceled our rooms and put our money together to help the one girl out," I told her. "Otherwise she would have had to go to a different resort and waste her whole trip. That wouldn't have been right."

"Okay . . ." Deidre was a little calmer. "Why did you have to cancel your room? Why couldn't the broke girl just stay with the other girl in her room?"

I exhaled as I thought about what to respond. I couldn't tell Deidre that I brought up the idea so that I wouldn't miss out on sleeping with two beautiful women. That would have confirmed her allegations. Damn, now I see how my exes felt when I used to put them in situations like this.

"EXACTLY! You don't have anything to say! Because I'm right! You're probably the one who recommended y'all all stay together! Now you're stuck in the middle of the ocean! That's what you get! You can drown for all I care!" *Click.*

"Hello? Deidre? Hello?" I took the phone away from my ear and looked at the screen. She had hung up on me.

I didn't know what to think. Should I be mad, feel bad or care less? We weren't a couple, so technically I had no obligations to her. If I wanted to share a room with two women or a hundred it was not her concern. On that note, I concluded that the girl was just crazy. I wasn't going to call her back. Instead I was going to get me a drink. I needed to take the edge off and make my fears of living on water for the next three days disappear.

Sheryl

I was standing on the deck gazing out into the lagoon when I heard someone walk past. I turned around to see one of my weekend roommates heading toward the room door.

"You headed out?" I asked.

She turned around, somewhat startled. "Oh, my God. You scared me."

"Sorry."

"It's okay. I didn't know you were out there," she said, oddly keeping from looking in my direction.

"Is everything okay?" I asked.

She nodded. "Yeah. I'm just terrified of the water. Can you close the curtain until I leave?"

That explains it, I thought. I stepped off the deck and back into the room, closing the curtains behind me.

"Ohhh," I said. "Well I guess sharing this room wasn't such a good idea after all then, huh?"

"It's cool. Long as I don't look out any windows and keep plenty of alcohol, I should be good," she said.

I chuckled. "I know that's right. But it's too bad 'cause the views are heavenly. You're missing out."

"Take pictures for me," she joked, turning the knob on the door.

I chuckled again. "Are you going anywhere near the front desk?"

"I'm going to the bar. So if that's by the front desk then yeah."

"Could you get me a calling card? I'll give you the money," I said, going toward my room to get my bag.

"You don't need a calling card. You can use my phone. I have an international plan. Unlimited."

"You sure? I don't wanna hold your phone hostage."

"I don't have anybody important calling me. Plus, I'm just going to get a drink and coming right back," she took her iPhone from her black Louis Vuitton damier speedy and lightly tossed it to me.

"Thank you. I appreciate it."

"No problem. You want something from the bar?"

I shook my head, "Naah."

"Okay." She left.

I walked back out on the deck and started dialing Ramona. I wanted to let her know I was in Tahiti safely and thank her again for sending me there in the first place.

Before I could push the last number, the phone started vibrating in my hand. It was an incoming call from Dee. I was going to ignore it but then I figured the least I could do was tell the caller that Angie went to the front desk and would be right back. Maybe it was one of her loved ones wanting to make sure she got here safe.

"Hello," I answered.

"Hello? Who is this?"

"I'm Sheryl. Angie went downstairs. She'll be right back though. You want me to tell her you called?"

"She got bitches answerin' her phone now too?" the woman mumbled.

"Excuse me?" I had to double-check if I had heard her correctly.

"I SAAAIDDDD," she was much louder and clearer, "SHE GOT BITCHES ANSWERIN' HER

PHONE NOW! YOU KNOW WHAT, TELL HER DON'T WORRY ABOUT CALLIN' ME BACK…"

"Um, I think you have the wrong impression," I tried to clear things up. I didn't want Sheryl to regret letting me use her phone and I damn sure didn't want the woman calling to think I was a lesbian.

"NO! I THINK YOU HAVE THE WRONG IMPRESSION! SEE ANGIE OUT THERE PLAYIN' LIKE SHE SINGLE TRYIN' TO BE THE SHOULDER FOR Y'ALL MISERBALE BITCHES TO CRY ON ALL THE WHILE SHE REALLY JUST TRYIN' TO BE THE LAP Y'ALL PUSSIES FALL IN! SHE AIN'T SLICK! WATCH'ER! AND TELL ALL THE REST OF THEM LONELY GIRLS DOWN THERE TO WATCH OUT FOR HER, TOO!"

I didn't know whether to laugh or cry listening to the obviously scorned woman go off on the other end of the phone. I wanted to tell her she needed to be on the trip, too, with all the trust issues she apparently had. But I didn't. I just let her vent. I was stuck on the fact that one of the women I was going to be sharing a room with this weekend was a lesbian. No wonder she proposed this idea, I figured. Now I needed to be on my toes. I made a mental note not to shower, undress, or do anything enticing in front of her.

"Okay, miss, honey . . ." I tried getting a word in, "I'm gonna hang up now and when Angie comes back in the room I will tell her you called. Okay?" I pressed the end button.

I had heard enough. The drama did not compliment my therapeutic vacation. Besides, all the insults were bound to have me arguing with the girl like I had anything to do with the issues she had with Angie. So I cut the cancer.

I called Ramona like I intended to do from the start and midway through me telling her about the bizarre call from the girl Dee, the door to our suite opened. I quickly changed the subject.

"Yeah, so like I was saying, thank you so much for doing this for me. I'll take lots of pictures and I'll see you back in California."

"Okay, girl," Ramona laughed, getting the hint that the girl who was the center of our brief gossip session was back. "Have fun."

I hung up the phone and gave it to Angie. "Thanks," I told her. I didn't bother to tell her about the call she had received. I didn't feel like repeating the conversation and revisiting the negativity. Plus, I figured Angie would hear all about it at some point or another. In fact, I was sure she would.

She threw the phone in her bag with one hand and brought her martini glass to her lips with the other. "You're welcome, girl. I'm about to change and go out on the beach. You wanna come?"

"Ummm," I thought about laying out, soaking up the sun, and enjoying the breeze and how much better a nap that would be than in my closed-in room. "Yeah, I could go for some sun."

"I'll be ready in like a half," she said, retreating to her room.

"Okay." I went to my room and freshened up. I opted for a one-piece instead of a bikini. I didn't want Angie to get any ideas.

Walking out my room, I grabbed my beige and brown Jimmy Choo snake-embossed leopard print tote. Then I turned back around and went to the closet. I skipped over a few hangers and got to the one with my cover-ups on it. I grabbed a leopard print sarong, wrapped it around my waist, and headed back to the door.

"This should definitely eliminate any thoughts," I said to myself as I stood in front of the mirror looking my reflection over one last time before proceeding out the door.

Leslie

I awoke to the sound of thunderous laughter. I sat up in the plush King-sized bed forgetting where the hell I was. I removed my sleep mask and the ocean was staring me in the face through the floor to ceiling window directly in front of my bed. It hit me, I was in paradise. I looked at my watch anxiously, wondering how long I had slept and how much fun I had missed. It was six o'clock L.A. time so it was only three in Tahiti. I let out a sigh of relief. I still had much of the day left to enjoy.

I got out of the bed, went into the bathroom, brushed my teeth and washed my face. I was powdering my nose when the door flung open.

"Sleeping Beauty, you finally up!" Angie said, a smile on her face and a drink in her hand.

"Hope you're well-rested 'cause we 'bout to party!" Sheryl added, sipping her drink to keep it from spilling over.

At first I was looking at the two of them like they were crazy. Then I reached out and grabbed Sheryl's glass of reddish-pink alcohol infused liquid. "Let me help you with that," I said, putting the glass to my lips and gulping it down. Leaving just a swallow in the bottom of the glass I handed it back to her and asked, "Where the hell's the party?"

Sheryl and Angie fell out. They laughed so hard it made me start laughing -- that and the buzz I began to feel from whatever was in Sheryl's glass. We ordered room service -- appetizers and more drinks and had a little fiesta right there in the room. We ate, drank, laughed, and joked. It was like we were three silly unsupervised teenagers. And damn, it felt good. No stress, no drama, no men! It was the start of one hell of a weekend.

About an hour and a half later we pulled ourselves up from the cozy couch and lounge chair the three of us had been sitting on and forced ourselves to get ready for the dinner Dr. Anna had planned at six.

I showered, shampooed, blow-dried and styled my hair, did my makeup, put on a royal blue, one-shoulder Roberto Cavalli cocktail dress, a pair of gold Manolo Blahniks, and accessorized my wrist, ears, and fingers with yellow gold jewelry from Lorraine Schwartz's Diamond Monkey collection. A few sprays of Crystal Noir by Versace and a gold clutch and I was ready to dine some of my court-ordered hours of therapy the hell away.

Angie

Stepping foot into the hotel lobby felt like I had died and gone to titty heaven. There were at least thirty women at the meet-and-greet and the smallest cup size had to be a D. I had to keep telling myself "look into her eyes" during the icebreaker game Dr. Anna had us play. And it didn't help that I was still a little tipsy from all the drinking I had been doing since I arrived at the hotel. I was looser than I should have been among such a crowd.

After about ten or fifteen minutes of us playing, *Which Famous Divorcee am I*, Dr. Anna got our attention and led us to the banquet room where we would privately dine.

There were three big round tables covered in fine linen and set for what looked like a five course meal. Naturally Sheryl, Leslie and myself sat at the same table. The other women spread out between what seats were left at our table and the other two tables. Dr. Anna didn't sit anywhere; she stood in the middle of the room in front of all three tables. Once we were all seated, she commenced speaking.

"Good evening, ladies," she beamed with excitement.

Good evenings, hi's, and hellos came from the group in unison.

"Welcome to the Fourth Annual Dress Burning Ceremony. I am so delighted to see such a great turnout this year. This is our biggest group yet," she smiled.

Some sporadic claps briefly interrupted her. Then she continued, "I see a few faces who have been here before, one who was actually here last year . . ."

The group chuckled as a petite, blonde stood up and waved proudly.

"Hey, we're not here to judge," Dr. Anna said, playfully. Another group-wide chuckle ensued. "But for most of you this is your first time on this trip. And let me tell you not only are you in for some life changing experiences, but you are in for a good time!"

The group started to cheer.

"This weekend is about starting your lives anew. It's about accepting whatever happened to you in your past and rejecting it in the future. It's about letting go. Now, I'm going to give you all a brief history about this trip while the lovely wait staff brings out beverages and hors d'oeuvres."

On cue, waiters and waitresses emerged with pitchers of water and trays of finger foods that looked more like works of art.

"Four years ago I opened the doors to my own practice, a niche psychiatric office for women in troubled relationships who were lowering the quality of their lives. I thought that I would have an influx of clients lining up to pay for my help. After all, the statistics showed that in 60% of all divorce cases it is the woman who doesn't remarry, has a hard time even dating, and who seems to put her life on hold. I figured all the women from that 60% would be making appointments with me to see how they could get their lives back. Boy was I wrong."

Everybody giggled.

"I sat in my office alone for the first three weeks. No calls, not even from telemarketers. Now you know that's bad."

More giggles.

"So I started asking myself how can I get these women to seek my help? I mean, I was sure they knew they needed it. But maybe they didn't feel comfortable admitting it. Maybe they didn't want to tell their friends and family members that they were going to see a psychiatrist. Maybe they didn't even want to tell themselves that. But, what if they were to go on a woman's retreat? A vacation to help clear their minds and mend their hearts after the immense stress and strain of a divorce. That wouldn't sound so bad, would it? That would actually sound like fun. And family members and friends would likely encourage something like that rather than ridicule it like they may the idea of seeing a shrink." Dr. Anna was telling the story as if it were four years ago and she was in her office alone trying to figure out a way to draw clients.

"That's when I got the idea to do a trip. I chose a spa resort on a tropical island with amenities that I knew women would love. I put together an itinerary with therapeutic but fun activities and I started advertising it in hair and nail salons and spas . . ."

"What made you name it 'The Dress Burning Ceremony'?" one of the women called out.

"Well, one of the activities I thought of was to have each woman burn their wedding dress, or any item that would bring closure to their divorce or failed relationship. And it was actually my mom's idea for me to name the entire trip after that activity. She thought it would draw more attention than just calling it a woman's retreat."

There were some head nods in the group letting Dr. Anna know that they agreed. Meanwhile, I munched on lamb bites and zucchini wraps. Leslie opted for crab balls. And Sheryl was so engulfed in Dr. Anna's bio that she hardly touched the black bean bruschetta she asked for.

"So here I am four years and over two hundred clients later . . ." The women applauded including myself. "Helping women reclaim their lives one torched dress at a time!" Dr. Anna concluded.

The applause continued as Dr. Anna took her seat at the middle table. Appetizers were brought out soon after, along with our choice of iced tea or lemonade. Our soup or salad followed. And right before the main course came out, Dr. Anna had us participate in another exercise.

Back in the middle of the room, she gave the instructions. "Ladies, I want you to each take a dollar bill out of your purse, pocketbook, clutch or for some of you, your bras . . ."

"Hahahaha . . ." the room broke out into laughter as the women started taking one-dollar bills out.

Leslie was looking around the room with frustration written all over her face. I remembered that after she had given Sheryl her share of the room cost, she had no money left. I took an extra dollar from my swarovski crystal egg-shaped evening bag. I nudged Sheryl who was right beside me and put the dollar in her hand, nodding for her to give it to Leslie who was to her right.

She did. Leslie looked up at me and thanked me. Then she made it a point to loudly say, "I don't ever carry cash on me being as though this has no limit," waving the black American Express card that had gotten declined at check-in earlier.

Sheryl and I exchanged confused glances but didn't say anything. We dismissed Leslie's unnecessary, overly boastful gesture and turned our attention back to Dr. Anna.

"I want you to write the name of your ex-husband, fiancé, boyfriend, baby's father, or whomever in your life has caused you any pain or distress."

The women were quick to jot names on their dollar bills. Me, I was sitting there trying to recall anybody whose name deserved to be written on mine. Then it hit me. But instead of one name I wrote down several, *Us Weekly*, *Life and Style*, *People*, and *TMZ*.

"Okay," Dr. Anna said, "now while your main course is being served, listen for instructions on what to do with those dollars."

Right then a handful of extremely built and attractive men dressed in shirtless tuxedos began serving us our roast duck, salmon, or filet mignon.

"Now ladies, here's your chance to have those exes do something you always wanted them to do!" Dr. Anna exclaimed. "Shove those dollar bills down these men's g-strings and tell whoever's name is on your bill to SUCK IT!"

The women roared with laughter and cheers. I even had to laugh at that one. Dr. Anna was cutting up. And in a matter of minutes we would all be cutting up right along with her. After each woman was served, the strippers started performing, immediately coming out of their pants. And every time one of the women would shout out, 'Suck it' we knew that another dollar bill was going in one of the strippers' thongs.

Sheryl

I was trying to focus on the excitement at hand but the more I did the more I found myself thinking about the things that really made me happy.

Strippers weren't my thing. Nothing against them, but I never got what the fuss was about. I was the type who'd much rather been at home nestled in the arms of a man who loved me, watching our child put on a performance to our delight. A family movie, hugs, kisses and laughter. Play dates. Shopping. Singing. Gardening. Working out. Simplicity.

It was all running rampant in my mind. All the things that brought me joy and fulfillment. The things I had missed greatly. I felt myself getting emotional, on the borderline of breaking down. I tried to engage in the activities before me to take my mind off my past life.

I took another dollar bill out my evening bag. I scribbled Kenneth's name across George Washington's face. I handed it to Leslie. She smiled big and waved the dollar in the air. A tanned white guy with an eight pack danced his way over to her. He thrust his bottom half into her face as she placed the dollar between the elastic waistband of his thongs and the lower part of his pecks. In my mind I said, suck it, as I pictured Kenneth grinning maliciously the night he drove me to leave.

Didn't help any. In fact the visual of Kenneth spawned more thoughts. And before long I was reliving my wedding day. Vividly flashes of Eric popped in my head. His warm smile, and embracing eyes. The way he told me he loved me and the sincerity in every word. How he told me I was beautiful and worth a thousand heavens. And how angelic he appeared the moment I laid eyes on him at a charity softball game Ramona dragged me to. I wished I'd never met him.

Leslie

This is my kind of dinner, I thought as Chip and Dale replicas paraded around me. I'm goin' to need more dollars. "One more. Put it on my tab," I yelled across the table to Angie, my supplier for the night.

She placed another dollar bill in my hand while delivering the bad news. "It's my last one."

"You're out of cash, too?"

"Out of dollars."

"What you got?" I asked.

"Two fifties."

"Give me one. I'll pay it all back."

"Are you serious? You're really going to put fifty dollars down that man's draws? You know how many drinks you can get with that?"

"A hard man does to me what a stiff drink does to you," I told her.

"Well in that case," she pulled a fifty out her purse. "Have fun!"

We both laughed as the money changed hands. Angie was a cool chick I was learning. I didn't mind hanging out with her at all. Now that Sheryl, she was a different story. She was more reserved, timid even. I didn't know what it would take to loosen that girl up.

I waved the fifty directly at Adam, my newfound friend. He pumped his pelvis the whole way to me, my eyes following every pump. It was like he was hypnotizing me with his penis.

I bent my forefinger up and down, motioning for him to lower his head. I whispered in his ear, "Can you change this fifty?"

He responded by straddling my lap, pulling his thong down far enough for me to see the top part of his manhood where his pubic hair would have begun had he not waxed it off. The dollars he had been given were no longer secure as they fell loose in his lap. Grinding back and forth, he used his body to transfer the dollars from his lap to mine.

I gathered the money, counting forty-nine. Then I wrapped my arms around his waist placing the fifty in the back of his thong. I gave his ass cheek a slap and he slowly rose from my lap. He licked his lips and backed away from me, still dancing to the thumping beat.

My panties were soaked as I imagined him penetrating me with that hard piece of dick he had just rubbed up and down my thighs. I need a cigarette.

Angie

It was weird at first, us sitting and eating while half naked men gyrated in front of us. But then it turned fun. As we all sipped down our wine and got comfortable telling people who did us wrong to suck it, we started to get riled up. Dr. Anna had unleashed the beast within each of us beauties and we were ready to party.

The drinks kept coming, the strippers kept dancing and the women were thinking of more and more people to tell to suck it, including Leslie, who had wounded up borrowing another fifty from me. She started writing down names of guys from as far back as high school. And each of her dollars went down the same stripper's draws. I secretly bet Sheryl that Leslie was going to find a way to get with him that night. Sheryl, a bit naïve, took the bet, claiming that Leslie, like the rest of the women, was just feeling good about releasing.

"Shittt," I told her. "She's thinking about how good it's gonna feel when *he's* releasing," I joked.

She smirked and shook her head. Then she sipped the last of her wine and stood up from the table. Looking down at Leslie and me, she said, "I think I'm going to go back to the room now. I'm tired."

"You sure? You want me to walk you?" I asked, concerned about the sudden mood change in Sheryl.

"No, that won't be necessary. I'm fine."

"Well don't wait up!" Leslie burst out as she stuffed another dollar down the underwear of what turned out to be her personal entertainer.

Sheryl smirked and told the table of women good night. She then left the restaurant in haste.

I hoped she was okay like she'd claimed. I thought about whether or not I should have accompanied her and made sure, but then I figured she must had needed some alone time.

I continued sipping and enjoying the entertainment well into dessert. It was then that the strip show was over and the men collected all their dollars and their pants and said their farewells. Our original wait staff served us our cheesecake or chocolate mousse and coffee, tea, or water. And the energy in the room slowly declined back to normal.

We all indulged in our final course as we snickered and carried on small talk about the surprise Dr. Anna had just given us. All except for Leslie who had excused herself right after the strippers left. She claimed she had to use the restroom. I knew better.

The evening winded down. The meet and greet dinner was over. We all thanked Dr. Anna for such a fun and empowering first day. We were told that there was an optional yoga session in the morning followed by a mandatory group lunch. I made up my mind right then and there I would skip yoga. I had plans on sleeping as late as I could.

"Like I thought," I mumbled under my breath, referring to the absence of Leslie in the ladies room. "Looks like I won the bet." I washed my hands and moistened them with the complimentary packet of hand cream. Took my lipstick-sized perfume out my purse and spurted a little on my neck and wrist. Lastly, I refreshed my gloss.

Lisa Wu Hartwell
and Miasha

As I exited the bathroom, I blended in with the other women who were retreating back to their rooms. But instead of calling it a night, I walked over to the bar and took a seat, coincidentally next to the woman who had raised her hand when Dr. Anna mentioned she saw someone who had been there last year.

As soon as I sat down she smiled at me. I smiled back.

"What are you drinking?" she asked me instantly.

I reluctantly answered, "A dirty martini."

She then got the attention of the bartender and ordered my drink for me.

"Extra dirty," I added to the bartender.

"Oooh . . . I like the sound of that," the woman said to me.

I thought I was tripping at first. Was I drunk or was this lady coming at me?

"Are you . . ?" I decided to just ask.

A huge grin on her face, she nodded and said, "Why do you think I'm back for a second year? I found more beautiful women here last year than I've found in all of L.A. the past seven years that I lived there."

I laughed. What were the odds of that, I thought. There was someone on that trip for the same reason I was and I just happened to sit next to her at the bar. It was looking like Leslie wouldn't be the only one of us getting some that night.

Sheryl

A t the sound of the bungalow door opening, I hurried and tossed the tissues that were scattered across the bathroom sink. Grabbing one more piece off the half-used roll I patted the corners of my eyes and blew my nose one final time. I threw the tissue in the toilet and decided to do the same with the others. I picked up the small trashcan and emptied it into the toilet. I flushed.

Looking at myself in the mirror right before turning out the light and leaving the bathroom, I hoped whoever it was who'd come in was not out in the hall. It was evident I had been crying my eyes out and I didn't feel like being questioned, nor comforted.

I opened the door slowly and peeped out. The coast was clear. I tiptoed into my bedroom.

"Huhhhh?" I gasped, startled at the shadowy figure sitting on my bed in the dark.

"Damn, did I scare you?" Angie's voice came from the figure.

"Oh my God, yes. What are you doing in here? Shouldn't you be passed out in your bed?" Neglecting to turn on the light, I walked over toward my bed, using my feet to clear the path of the clothes and shoes I had taken off hours before.

"I peeped in to check on you and saw you were up. You okay?"

"I'm fine." I climbed in my bed on the opposite side of where Angie was sitting. "You need to go to bed. We got a lot on our schedule for tomorrow."

"You sure?"

"Yeah, yoga first thing in the morning and then the . . ."

"No. Are you sure you're fine? You don't sound like it."

"I'm just tired."

Angie stood up and walked toward the door. I assumed she got the hint. But when she pushed the light switch it was apparent she didn't.

I tried to pull the covers over my face before Angie could see my puffy, mascara-smeared eyes but my reaction was too slow.

"You been crying," Angie discovered.

I turned over in the bed, my back to Angie. "It's nothing, Angie. Go to bed."

Angie made her way back to sitting on the edge of my bed. Putting her hand on my shoulder, she asked, "What's wrong, Sheryl?"

"Nothing," I persisted. "Just late night thoughts."

"About what? The reason you're here?"

Finally I turned around to give Angie what she was looking for. "I miss my daughter," I confessed.

"Well, where is she?"

I felt a rush of emotion as I tried to cage the tears that were welling in my eyes. "She's in foster care now." The tears broke free.

Angie leaned down and put her arms around me as I sobbed.

"Why is she in foster care? You seem like a perfect mother," Angie was forcing me to talk.

"I was. I am. But him and his team of high-powered lawyers made it look totally different in front of the judge."

"Your Honor, she left home for two weeks without so much as a phone call to check on her daughter to say hello, to let her know that she was okay. She is now living in an apartment. She has no job, no income, no savings. Nothing. She has no way to get her daughter to and from the private school she attends which is close to the child's current residence with her father. And furthermore, she is emotionally unstable to care for a child at this time. For these reasons, we are asking that our client be granted temporary custody of the child."

"The judge saw it their way. And even the court-appointed lawyer I had saw it their way. So I was in a no-win situation."

Angie took her arms from around me, her face wrinkled, she asked, "How the hell did you end up with a court-appointed lawyer and he had a power team?"

"I couldn't afford a lawyer," I wiped my eyes. "And an attorney friend of mine was going to represent me but my ex-husband paid him off to walk away from the case and mind his business."

"Well, it's obvious to me that you two were pretty wealthy."

"HE was wealthy," I corrected her.

"I ain't never been married before but I do know that once a woman marries a man, what's his becomes hers."

"Not if you sign a prenup."

"WHAT?! Tell me you did not sign a prenup!"

"It was never about the money to me. Besides, I had my Masters Degree when I met him and was a professor at UCLA teaching screen writing classes. I had my own money, my own house, my own cars. I never expected to need anything from him. Then once we got married he wanted me to stop working, sell my house and my cars. Move into his mansion with him, drive the better cars that he brought me, and focus on being a good wife and a potentially good mother to the children he wanted to have with me right away."

"And so you gave up your entire life for this man and trusted in his word to always take care of you?"

I nodded.

"Which is exactly why you shouldn't have signed no prenup! I mean, think about it. You gave up your independence for this man and put your well-being in his hands. You trusted in his word that he would take care of you. Yet, he didn't trust your word that it was not about the money and he had you sign some shit? If anything he should've signed something stating that he would uphold his promise to you so that you would never be in the position you're in now! That's some bullshit. I need a drink."

Angie got up and stormed out the room. I heard glasses clanking from the mini-bar.

"You want one?" she yelled to me.

"No . . ."

"Well, you need one!"

She reentered my room carrying two cups filled halfway with a clear liquid.

"So, if your husband was granted custody why is your daughter in foster care now?" she asked, handing me the additional cup.

I sat up in the bed, resting my back against the headboard. "My husband is in jail."

"For what?"

"He murdered my fiancé at our wedding," I gulped the drink.

"WHAT?! That's sick! Oh my God! I'm sorry to hear that."

"It's like he has managed to fuck me over every which way he could. And to this day he still has control over me, and over anything I do. That's why I can't live my life, because every turn I make he's right there reminding me that I am nothing without him," I vented.

"Reminds me of my stalker," Angie muffled. "Why are men so got damn crazy and controlling?"

"You have a stalker?" I turned the floor over to her.

"Yeah. Some crazy ass actor broke into my house and chased me around naked because I didn't choose him for a role. I'm not even a casting agent. I'm a damn director!"

"That's absurd. I hope he didn't think you would give him the role after that."

Angie drank her drink.

"What happened? Did he catch you," I couldn't help but chuckle.

Angie chuckled too and said, "Thank God my friend was there. She snuck up behind him and knocked him over the head with . . ." Angie just stopped talking.

I looked over at her and she was staring into space. "With what?" I asked.

Her voice lowered and even cracked as she whimpered, "My vase . . . My one of a kind chocolate diamond encrusted vase all the way from Sierra Leone -"

"Wow, must have been expensive huh?"

"Cost me two cars. And I'm not talking Fords either," Angie took the rest of her drink back. "You want another one?" she asked, getting up, headed to the mini bar.

I shook my head. I couldn't take another. Upon coming back into my room with her 'I don't know what number' drink, Angie continued where she left off.

"Honestly, though, I was just thankful Dee was there. She saved my life."

"Dee?"

"My friend."

Dee, that name rang a bell. "Oh she's the one who called your phone earlier with the jealous girlfriend traits," I let the cat out the bag.

Angie's head spun around so fast she could have gotten whiplash. "She did? When?"

"When you let me hold your phone. She thought you and I had something going on because I had answered your phone. I tried to explain to her that that wasn't the case. But she was not tryin' to hear that."

"Oh my God. Why didn't you tell me?"

"I just thought she'd tell you once you two talked. I didn't want to stir up any drama."

"Girl, you should've told me. I would've called her and put her in her place."

"So she's not your girlfriend?" I inquired.

"I'm not a lesbian!" Angie became defensive.

"You're not?"

"Why is that a surprise?"

"Well, you seem like you could be one and then the phone call from your," I made quotation marks with my fingers, "friend."

Angie picked up a pillow and tossed it at me gently. "She is just my friend! What are you tryin' to say?"

"O-kay whatever you say," I teased. Obviously Angie didn't want me to know her sexual preference yet. I didn't push either. I was just happy that conversing with her had made me feel somewhat better. I was coming up out of my slump.

Leslie

"**B**itches, I'm home," I sang as I walked into my shared suite carrying my shoes in my hand. It was a quarter to three in the morning. Yet I was feeling wide-awake. I felt like I was floating on cloud nine actually. I was bubbly and giggly, the way I always felt after good sex.

I stopped in my room to drop off my shoes and bag and then proceeded down the hall to the alcove where Angie and Sheryl's rooms were tucked away. I gave a soft knock on Angie's door. No answer. I opened it a little just to see if she was in there. She wasn't. Hmmm, I thought.

I tapped on Sheryl's door next. No answer. I cracked open her door to be hit in my face with a barrage of pillows.

"Got you!" the two of them squealed as they slapped hands and shared a laugh.

I just grinned as I joined them on Sheryl's bed. "It's goin' to take more than some pillows to knock me out the sky."

"Ummm," Angie moaned. "That must've been some real good, hot, steamy stuff," she exxagerated.

"Girl," I couldn't stop smiling. "That's all I can say."

Angie held out her palm and on cue Sheryl got up and walked over to the armoire that was against a wall a few feet from her bed. She opened the doors and took her clutch out. She took a twenty-dollar bill from it and slammed it in Angie's hand. I caught on instantly. "Y'all hussies took a bet out on me?"

"Angie called it," Sheryl said.

"Hell with y'all!" I said playfully. "What are y'all doin' up anyway? I had plans on coming in here and annoying y'all."

"Chile, we been up talking and drinking," Angie told me.

"Talking about what?" I was nosy.

"About crazy men and what brought us here."

"Ohhhh," I sighed. "Like I wanna go down that path tonight. I'll end up ready to jump in the fuckin' ocean if I have to think about that two-timing liar!"

"Is he the one who took all your money?" Sheryl asked, innocently.

"My money, my sanity, my freedom, my happiness, my security!" I ran it down.

"Who was he? Your husband?"

"He would have been. But while I was at the altar, he was at the hospital coaching his pregnant wife through the delivery of their third child."

"Oh my." Sheryl was surprised.

"Men, men, men. I tell you," Angie said. "That's just why . . ." Then she stopped herself.

Sheryl grinned and looked up at her. "Why what?" she asked Angie.

Angie paused then she stood up and held court. "Why I'm a damn lesbian! There! I said it!"

"Whaaaat?" I laughed. "Where did that come from?"

"She tried to deny it earlier," Sheryl caught me up.

"Deny it how? It's right there in black and white on page 46 of Us Weekly. It's the reason she stood Bobby

Fuller up at the altar!" I recounted what I had read earlier on the plane.

"Oh, so you knew?" Sheryl asked me.

"Yeah, me and the rest of the country," I answered. "Are you one, too?" I asked Sheryl.

"No, no, no," Sheryl assured me.

"Oh. I was about to say, I'm surrounded," I laughed.

Angie sat back down and said, "I don't care that everybody knows anymore. It's actually less stressful now that I know for sure who I am and what I want."

"Yeah, I bet," I said. "So will you be burning a dress or a tux tomorrow night?" I was sarcastic, but curious.

After we all laughed Angie answered, "Neither. I'll be burning all those damn magazines that you were reading on the plane."

We shared another laugh. Angie then got up. "I'm going to refill. You want a drink Leslie?"

I shrugged. "Sure. I can use something to bring me down."

Angie looked at Sheryl as if to ask if she wanted a drink. Sheryl shook her head and Angie walked out of the room.

"How many has she had?" I whispered.

"I lost count," Sheryl whispered back.

"She better be careful. She goin' be a lesbian alcoholic. And that is not a cute combination. Can you imagine somebody licking you down there and all you can smell is alcohol on their breath?"

"Illll," Sheryl shrieked.

"Yuck," I added.

"Can I ask you a question?" Sheryl quizzed.

"What?"

"Why are you seeing Dr. Anna? You seem like such a strong woman who has it all together."

"I am. It was court ordered. I didn't have a choice."

"Why did the court order you to see a shrink?"

"You know that song," I cleared my throat and sang, *"I bust the windows outcha car . . ."*

Sheryl smiled, "Jazmine Sullivan."

"I took that song to heart. Wound up getting locked up and it was between anger management or one-on-one. I can't stand school so the idea of a class was out the window. Dr. Anna it was."

"You were in jail before?" she was inquisitive.

"Well, not like in jail in jail, like how my brother is. He's sitting. I just got arrested."

"Why's your brother in jail?"

"Something stupid. He got high one night and broke into some Hollywood director's house naked trying to audition for a role in his movie," I chuckled at the stupidity of my brother's shameless act.

"You said, 'in *his* movie'? So, the director was a man?"

"Yeah," I thought about it, "Well, I guess. My brother just said director. I figure all Hollywood directors are men, right? Anyway, I'm tryin' to get him out of there before my grandmother croaks."

"Oh goodness," Sheryl said.

Then Angie walked in with our drinks.

"You're right on time," I said reaching for my cup. "Thinking about my dumb ass brother got me needing a drink."

"What about your brother?" Angie asked me.

Then Sheryl interrupted as if she didn't want to hear the story about my brother again. I didn't blame her. "Ladies, can we finish our girl talk in the morning? I'm exhausted. And I have to get up for yoga in a couple hours."

"You're going to yoga?" I asked.

"I would like to. That's one of the things I used to love to do. Keeps me centered."

"Oh. Well, I'll see y'all at lunch, if I even make it there," I said, getting up off Sheryl's bed.

"It's mandatory, Leslie," Angie reminded me. "Don't you need those hours?"

I turned back to look at Angie, "You're so right. I have to stay focused. I can't let another dick take me off my square."

The girls laughed and Angie shouted out, "Suck it!" mocking Dr. Anna at dinner earlier.

I joined in their laughter as I carried my drink and myself to bed.

Angie

"Oh Godddddd. Ugh," I tried to roll over but was tangled in the comforter. My head was pounding and the pain worsened whenever I so much as cracked open my eyelids. I lay there tightly snuggled in a cocoon wishing I could kick myself in the ass for drinking so much the night before.

I forced my eyes open to read the time on my cell phone screen. "Owwwch," I whined as I struggled to read the tiny numbers. Everything was a blur and made me dizzy. I was miserable. Giving up after a few seconds, I detangled myself and turned over to look at the clock on the nightstand beside the bed.

Opening and shutting my eyes repeatedly I tried to make out the digital numbers. It was all zigzagged to me. "Ugh!"

I picked up my phone and pressed the number two to speed dial Deidre. It was her fault I was in this shitty situation. Had she never forced her tongue down my throat, I wouldn't have ever been confused about my sexuality and would have gone on to marry Bobby Fuller. My career would still be intact, my drinking under control, and I would surely not be in Tahiti at a dress burning ceremony!

"Oh shit! The ceremony! It's tonight!"

"Hello?" Deidre's voice interrupted my rants.

"Deidre."

"What Angie?" she groaned.

"What time is it?" I asked, bypassing her attitude toward me.

"You called me to ask me the time?"

"No. But now that I have you on the phone, I'd like to know." I was trying to remain cool but she was seconds from having me go off on her.

"Nine-twenty, why?"

Calculating the three hour time difference, I muffled under my breath, "So it's eight, seven, six-twenty here. Okay. I got a hour to get myself together," I thought aloud.

"Um, excuse me! I know you didn't call me to plan out your day! That's the selfish shit I'm talking about!" Deidre spat.

"No! I called you to curse you the hell out for putting my business out there to a stranger!" I got back to the original reason for my call.

"What business of yours did I put out? What are you talking about? You must be drunk!"

"I am drunk! And I got a crazy hangover so I'm really not in the mood for your bullshit but since you insist I feed into the drama, here it goes! You called my phone and acted a fool to my roommate who was just being nice by taking a message for me!"

"Oh her? Please, I ain't hardly act a fool. Is that what she told you? Tell her if she wanna see me act a fool I'll show her actin' a fool!"

"Too late! And as a matter of fact I'm tired of seeing you act a damn fool! I thought we could go back to being friends but now I see that you can't handle that! Let's call it quits okay? Lose my number and I'll lose yours!"

"BIT . . ."

Click. I ended the call before Deidre could get the bitch out her mouth. Immediately after, I had an incoming call from her. I turned my phone off. I didn't feel like going back and forth with her. That would do nothing but make my headache worst; and besides, I needed to get myself together to go the ceremony that was scheduled to start at seven thirty.

I forced myself up out the bed and into the shower. Standing under the rainwater showerhead and allowing the hot water to pour over my face and down my body, I started to come alive. I washed up, dried off, and called down to the front desk for some Aspirin. I ordered room service, too; a cheeseburger on a sourdough roll and a side of fries.

By the time I threw on my navy and white striped D&G jumpsuit and red Alexander McQueen's, a silver tray was being rolled in my room. I signed my name on the receipt and sent the young island guy on his way.

I gorged the food like a hostage. Taking the two pills after a few bites, I downed the cranberry juice. Brushed my teeth, applied my makeup, grabbed a handful of tabloid magazines and my room key and headed out the door.

Leslie

"Right here, right here," I instructed the bellhop as he pushed the luggage cart with my wedding dresses.

I removed my Louboutin heels and trekked through the sand toward the bonfire where Dr. Anna and her group of clients and friends were. I was impressed at the set-up. It looked like a beach wedding with rows of chairs facing the water. I expected that we'd gather around a fire, toss our baggage in the flames, and keep it moving. But in Dr. Anna fashion, the dress burning ceremony was a real damn ceremony. She had a DJ, hors d'oeuvres, champagne and everything, much more than I had imagined.

"Thank you," I politely told the bellhop as he laid the large Louis Vuitton garment bag across my arms.

He paused before taking the luggage cart back into the lobby of the hotel. I wished I had cash to tip him. He certainly deserved it. It was rough maneuvering the cart through the sand. But unfortunately all I could give him was a smile. He got the picture and walked away.

All heads turned in my direction as I took a seat in the back row next to Sheryl. I felt compelled to explain my tardiness.

"I'm sorry I'm late. I had to wait for the front desk to send someone up with a luggage cart."

"I was wondering where you and Angie were," Sheryl whispered.

"I was saying good-bye to my Chip and Dale friend," I whispered back with a wink. "Angie's probably still in bed."

"Not a problem," Dr. Anna voiced from front and center, "We're still waiting for one more. But you do know this is a *dress* burning ceremony not an ex-husband burning ceremony . . .My God, is that a garment bag or a body bag?" she joked.

The other ladies chuckled as they all looked at me, waiting for my response.

"As much as I would love to have his body in here, I don't. It's this big because there are three dresses in it," I explained.

The chuckle turned into laughter and Dr. Anna asked, "You're burning three dresses tonight?"

I nodded. "Yeah, only three. The fourth one wouldn't fit."

The laughter grew louder and lingered longer.

"Oh that's funny," Dr. Anna crackled.

But what was funny was that I wasn't joking. I had been married twice before and almost married twice before. So I really did have four wedding dresses. Shit, I could have opened my own bridal shop.

"Well it's better to have four wedding dresses than four divorce decrees," one of the women called out.

"Wedding dresses, divorce decrees…it's all the same to me. They both become ashes when you toss them in a fire," I said, nonchalantly.

Another burst of laughter came from the ladies. I felt like a damn comedian.

"You are crazy," Sheryl muffled, prompting me to look her over.

"Where's your dress?" I asked, noticing her lap was one of the few that was void a gown.

"My issues are deeper than a dress," she stated.

I glanced back at her lap and saw pictures and what looked like ultrasound photos. I started to ask to see them, but Dr. Anna snatched my attention.

"Okay we can get started now that our final guest is here," she said, her eyes following Angie as she pep-walked to the seat beside me.

Angie sat down seemingly embarrassed. "I apologize," she said simply.

"You all right?" I asked.

"Why y'all ain't wake me up?" she complained.

"I tried to wake you up and you told me to leave you the hell alone."

"That was seven o'clock this morning for yoga," she said.

"No, it wasn't. It was eleven for the mandatory lunch!"

"Shhh," Sheryl tapped my knee, bringing Angie and my back and forth to a halt.

"Good evening, ladies," Dr. Anna greeted the group. "Welcome to the Fourth Annual Dress Burning Ceremony. Tonight marks the night where each of you will officially burn the past and light a torch for the future. The way this works is that you will each come up one at a time and recite the vows I helped you all write . . ."

"What vows?" Angie whispered.

"The vows we wrote at the *mandatory* lunch that I tried to wake you up for," I sassed.

Sheryl cleared her throat as a gesture to get Angie and me to shut up. She thought she was our mom, I swear.

". . . Then you will place your dress or whatever item you have in the fire. From there you will take your seat. Any questions?"

I raised my hand.

"Yes, Leslie?"

"Can I go first?" I asked. "I wanna get this over with."

"Sure, I was just about to ask for a volunteer. Come on up."

I stood up and slid past Sheryl, which was more difficult than it would have been, had I not been lugging an oversized garment bag.

I could feel the women's eyes roaming up and down my body, most likely checking out my attire, as I walked down the rose-pedaled aisle.

"Okay, let's hear it," Dr. Anna coached.

"I, Leslie DiRosa, promise to dispose of all thoughts, ideas, wishes, and dreams . . . whether wet or dry . . ." I paused until the ladies stopped laughing, then proceeded, "of being with Frank Gastin. I promise to love and to cherish myself above all and not allow Frank or any man to dictate what I do with my life. I will live for me and for people who genuinely love me from this day forth."

"Woohoo!" the ladies cheered as they applauded.

Clapping and smiling Dr. Anna took it upon herself to clarify, "I didn't have anything to do with that wet or dry dream part."

"That was all me," I cosigned. I took a step over toward the fire. I lifted the garment bag up off my arms and held it out.

"Aren't you gonna remove them from the bag?" Dr. Anna inquired.

"What for?" I shrugged, tossing the entire bag into the flames.

"IT WAS A LOUIS!" a woman's voice shrieked from the crowd.

"It was bought with his money," I said, carefree. I took a cigarette from my purse and lit it with the engulfed flames as the DJ played *Burn Baby Burn, Disco Inferno, Burn Baby Burn* . . . in the background.

Puffing and doing the bump with Dr. Anna, I felt like a burden had been lifted off me. It was as if I had been set free from bondage. Who knew that what I had placed so much value on throughout my life was in turn causing me to place less value on myself? I was trading me for money and the finer things in life. And now that I was giving those things up, I was getting me back. At that moment I embraced Dr. Anna. Her little trip changed my whole outlook on life.

**Lisa Wu Hartwell
and Miasha**

Angie

I had gotten away with letting women go before me long enough. When no one was no longer volunteering, Dr. Anna's eyes shot straight back to me.

"Angie, would you like to go next?"

"I guess," I sighed, standing up. I took my handful of weekly magazines to the front.

"Tell everybody what you have there," Dr. Anna suggested.

I held one of the magazines up and stated the obvious, "Tabloid magazines."

The sounds that rumbled from the women made me feel all the more uncomfortable. Clearly they were wondering why the hell I was burning magazines. I was asking myself the same question. I mean, I didn't belong at the ceremony and I felt so out of place. All the women before me went up and recited vows of ending their marriages -- some after twenty years and here I was complaining about some damn rumors and exaggerated truths. I should have been ashamed of myself. I was wasting everybody's time. And on top of it, I didn't have any vows to recite. It had seemed that I had come there just to take advantage of the free drinks and vulnerable women. I couldn't feel more selfish.

"You want to explain why you're burning magazines," Dr. Anna asked.

114

I hesitated then I shook my head. "I don't know my damn self. To be honest I don't think I need to be here…"

Gasps of confusion circulated so I further explained, "Unlike you all, I've never been married. Never even been in a real serious, long-term relationship. I came here for the wrong reasons and," I glanced at Dr. Anna, "I feel bad that I've wasted your time." I started to walk back up the aisle and Dr. Anna stopped me in my tracks.

"Angie."

I turned to face her.

"You're doing it all over again," she said, shaking her head.

"Doing what?"

"Don't you see it? It's a pattern. You go through with the whole process and wait until you get to the altar to expose yourself," she broke it down. "Why do you think you do this to yourself?"

I looked at Dr. Anna, almost staring. "You know what Dr. Anna, that's a good damn question and I don't have an answer to it."

She was right. This was a pattern of mine. I never even noticed it. Even before the wedding, I would do things like this. One time in school I rehearsed three times a week faithfully for a play and opening night I went out on the stage and instead of delivering my lines, I confessed to the audience that I didn't know why I was up there. I really wanted to direct the play not act in it. I had no business being Juliet. Someone who really wanted the role should have gotten it. Not me. I was wrong and I was sorry. And here I was doing the same thing again tonight.

"Well maybe this is just what you needed to find the answer. Maybe you do need to be here."

I remained silent.

"Something inside you tells you you're not deserving of certain things. It's like the angel on one shoulder and the devil on the other. You seem to struggle with those distinct voices. Like on the one hand you're being told you can do it, this is what you want, this is what you need. Then right when you're about to take the step here comes that devil asking 'What are you doing? Are you crazy? This isn't what you want. You don't need this. You're wasting everybody's time.' And you give in to that final voice -- that voice wins every time," Dr. Anna summed up.

I was awestruck. Dr. Anna had read me so thoroughly. Now all I needed to know was what the hell I was supposed to do about it.

"So, now that we know my issue, what's the prognosis?"

"Well if you don't start trusting your own voice, you're gonna short yourself out of so much of what's yours in this life."

"How do I trust my voice? I mean, how do I even hear it? And when I do hear it, how do I know it's my voice and not the devil's or the angel's?" I was extremely intrigued at that point. I wanted to know the solution to the problem that I had had for many years without even realizing it.

Dr. Anna hesitated. Then she instructed, "Come back up here and throw those magazines in the fire like you intended from the beginning. And afterward, listen."

I did just that. I tossed the magazines. I returned to my seat and while I sat listening to *Hit The Road Jack* something inside me said, Yes! I nodded and thought to myself, *That's what it was. I was never giving my own voice a chance. I kept letting the other voices cut mine short.*

Never again, I thought, *never again.*

Lisa Wu Hartwell
and Miasha

Sheryl

Dr. Anna was bringing about so many breakthroughs I was anxious to get up there and experience mine. It would mean so much to me if I could shed the skin I've grown over the course of my marriage that has caused me to completely lose myself. I would give anything to be the person I was before I met Kenneth. I was so different then. I was more fun, more relaxed, and just free. I had my own everything and what I didn't have I could get if I wanted. Kenneth was just an accessory. And somehow over the years I had allowed him to strip me of it all, down to my self worth. How, I didn't know. But what I did know was that I was fed up with it. I wanted my life back. And the way I saw it, it was now or never.

"Sheryl," Dr. Anna called me up to the front.

I rose from my seat and eagerly walked to the altar. I took a deep breath and recited my vows, "I, Sheryl Lee, wish that my ex-husband would burn in hell the way that these ultrasound pictures he brought home to me are about to burn in this fire --" I started choking up but I continued, "I will never forget the lie he made me live that wound up bringing me my greatest joy but yet my greatest pain . . ." I threw the pictures of my fake pregnancy into the flames and flashbacks of what I went through appeared in my mind with every crackle.

"I'm sorry Mr. and Mrs. Stewart, but Mrs. Stewart you do have endometriosis which very well could be

why you and your husband have been unable to conceive..."

The minute we left the doctor's office and got in the car he unleashed his fury, "What are we going to do? Huh?" he screamed.

"We're going to keep trying," I told him. "Anything is possible through God."

"Keep trying? For how much longer? What, you want me to be fifty years old having my first child?"

I wrapped my arms around him and he brushed me off mumbling, "I wish I would've known this shit."

I was devastated. I felt like my insides were ripped out of me. And all that was left was my outer shell. That was the day that I stopped feeling, believing, trusting, loving. That was the day it all went cold. I was a robot after that.

A couple months went by and he brought home some ultrasound pictures. He told me we were going to tell our family and friends that we were expecting a baby. He said he had already worked out a deal with a female friend. She agreed to let him impregnate her and once the baby was born he could have it. He would give her three hundred thousand dollars and she would walk away without mention of it ever happening.

"So, you went out and slept with somebody else?" I remember was my first concern.

"No, I gave up my sperm at one of those clinics! What the hell do you think I did?" he fumed. "Now this is the plan and you stickin' to it! You wanted a fuckin' baby right? RIGHT?"

Shaken with fear and misery, I nodded, fighting my tears with all my might. Only when he disappeared, did I break down. I was at an all time low. And ironically after going nine months pretending to be pregnant, stuffing my dresses with pillows and everything, it was *the welcoming of the baby girl that my husband had conceived with another woman that brought me the joy and love I had been lacking for years.*

It was hard, especially during the first few years. Looking at this baby grow, knowing she was someone else's. I loved her so much but sometimes looking at her brought up so much anger. It's a wonder I didn't lose my mind. Then there would be days that I would be so unhappy and it was like she could sense it. Even at two and three years old. She would wobble over to me with the warmest smile and say, 'I love you, mommy.' My heart would just melt. And I would know that she was in my life for a reason. She was my guardian angel.

"I felt like I couldn't live without her," I was back in the moment. "But now that we're divorced I'm being forced to. He made me look so incapable of taking care of her on my own. So now I have to either prove that that's not true or go the rest of my life without my baby girl," I broke down.

And I wasn't the only one. The whole group was in tears. Even Leslie, who before now appeared to be so unmoved by everything, had to excuse herself. Dr. Anna, Angie, and a few other women hugged me, allowing me to cry in their arms. The DJ stopped playing the background music and the ceremony seemed to come to a halt. It wasn't the breakthrough I was hoping for. Instead, it was another breakdown. And I had wondered if it was simply too late for me.

Leslie

It was Sunday, our final day of activities in Tahiti. I awoke to the sound of rumbling coming from the hallway. I glanced at the clock on the nightstand. It was only six in the morning. This was the one and only day Dr. Anna didn't have any early morning exercises planned so I wondered who was up and what the hell they were doing at that hour.

I got out of the bed and walked over to the door. I opened it as I called out, "Angie? Sheryl?"

No one responded. I grew suspicious as I walked out the room and crept down the hallway.

No one was in the living area or the kitchenette. But I did notice Sheryl's bedroom door was opened. And over the past two days she'd always slept with her door closed, as did we all.

I walked down to her room and looked inside. She was gone. Her closet was empty and so were her drawers. Her bed was neatly made, which didn't make sense to me. We had housekeeping, for crying out loud. I left the room and went back into the living area, rushing for the door to the suite.

I opened it and peeked down the hall. No one in sight. I went back inside and looked around. I noticed a piece of paper at the mini bar.

Dear Angie it read. "She put this note in the perfect place for Angie to find it," I chuckled. *Getting to know you this weekend was a blast. You helped make this trip fun for me. Thank you for listening and being a shoulder to cry on. I wish you well in your career and*

121

hope to stay in touch. It was signed Sheryl and had her cell number at the bottom.

At that I went to wake up Angie and let her know that Sheryl had left. I wondered if she knew why. I started to knock on Angie's door but I said what the hell and just cracked it open.

And boy did I regret that. "AHHH!" I screamed at the sight of Angie performing oral sex on one of the women in Dr. Anna's group. "Oh my God! I'm so sorry!" I shouted through the door that I had shut as quickly as I had opened it.

"LESLIE!" Angie yelled. "DON'T YOU HAVE ANY MANNERS?"

"I said I was sorry! Go back to doin' what you were doin'. I'll talk to you when you're done. Just make sure you brush your teeth!" I called out as I walked back down the hall. "And gargle, too, please!"

I went in the kitchen to make myself a cup of coffee. There was no way I would be able to go back to sleep after that. I was freaked out. The thought of licking a pussy gave me the creeps. I instantly got a nasty taste in my mouth. I needed a cigarette. Once my coffee was done, I went out on the deck to have me a smoke.

It wasn't even seven o'clock yet and Angie was up having sex. I thought I was wild, I said in my head as I walked out onto the deck.

I reached for the pack of Newports I kept on the patio furniture that was on our deck. It was my way of making sure I only smoked outside. Otherwise, I may have gotten kicked out of the nonsmoking suite.

There was a piece of paper wrapped securely around the pack. "This must be my *Dear John* letter," I mumbled. "Sheryl, you're a funny lady putting these notes in these places."

I unwrapped the paper. *Dear Leslie, What can I say? You are one of a kind. I am so glad your credit card got declined and I was able to spend the weekend with you. You were a ball of fun. I hope you got whatever help you came to get and please let's stay in touch. Sheryl. P.S. I left because there's something very important I want to take care of first thing in the morning. It had nothing to do with last night, or any of you. I am fine. Please pass this message on to Angie.*

I folded the letter back up and placed it on the table. I smoked my cigarette, drank my coffee, and enjoyed the early morning breeze.

I was nearly through my cigarette and still sipping my coffee when Angie joined me.

"How was breakfast?" I asked her sarcastically. She stepped out onto the deck backwards, her hands holding onto the walls on each side of the sliding doors.

"Better than that stale looking coffee," she dished back.

I just shook my head in an effort to remove the visual that popped in it.

"So, what did you want that was so important that you couldn't knock?" she asked, still facing the inside of the suite.

"Sheryl left," I said, blowing a ring of smoke out my mouth. "Why is your back turned?" I finally asked.

"I'm petrified of the water. You're lucky I'm even out here," she explained. "Now what were you saying about Sheryl leaving?"

I went to hand her the note Sheryl wrote me but realized the wind had gotten to it first. "Oh shit," I said. "My note flew away?" I wondered as I looked under the table.

What note? She wrote you a note?"

"Yeah, she wrote you one too. It's at your favorite spot."

"Where?"

"The bar."

"Oh, well, I guess she put yours in your ashtray," she predicted.

I couldn't help but snicker. "Close," I said.

"Well, what did it say?" she glanced sideways at me.

"She just was telling us how much she enjoyed getting to know us and that she left because she had something important to take care of tomorrow morning," I gave Angie Sheryl's notes in a nutshell.

"Oh. Well, I hope she'll be all right. 'Cause of all of us, she seemed to be the most hurt."

"Fuck hurt," I chimed in, "Whoever her husband was, he destroyed her," I evaluated.

I took the last puff on my cigarette and smashed the butt in the ashtray. "Men like that, who beat up on women, make me so sick. I wish I could gather them all up and set their asses on fire."

Angie

I was walking through LAX, my carry-on bag over one shoulder and my cell phone propped between the other and my ear. Leslie was beside me, pulling her Louis Vuitton rolling suitcase behind her.

"She's still not answering," I said, referencing Deidre. "I guess I'll just get a cab."

"You don't have to ride in a cab," Leslie said. "I'll take you home. It's no big deal," she offered.

"You sure?"

"Of course. All that you and Sheryl have done for me this weekend? Please, it's the least I can do."

"Well, how about with that hundred you owe me from Mr. Chip and Dale, you fill up your tank and we call it even?"

"I appreciate the gesture. But I'm not a complete charity case. I will pay you your money back *and* take you home."

We arrived at baggage claim, got the rest of our luggage and had a skycap place it all on a cart and push it outside to the curb. I waited with the luggage while Leslie took a shuttle bus to her car, which was parked in long-term parking.

I must have tried Deidre twenty more times while I waited for Leslie to pull up. I left messages and sent a few texts. She didn't respond to any of it. I must have really pissed her off that time. She usually called me back after one message. Now, she was avoiding me like a plague.

A custom white Range Rover Sport with red interior, a kitted grill and deep-dish white rims with red lining, pulled up in front of me.

That's when I noticed the emblems on the SUV were also painted red. This is some real diva shit, I remember thinking as I walked the skycap to the trunk and directed him where to put the bags. I wanted to make sure mine were on top, being as though I would be getting out first.

Leslie got out of the car right as I was tipping the guy and she intervened.

"I got it," she said, handing the guy a folded bill. He took it and thanked the both of us. Putting my money back in my pocketbook I shot Leslie a look like, 'Where did that come from?' She read the expression on my face correctly and volunteered, "I always keep a few hundred in cash in my car. You never know when you might need it."

"Well, hell you should've drove to Tahiti," I teased as I climbed in the passenger seat. "You had this lowered?" I asked immediately, noticing that I didn't have to use much effort getting into the SUV like I usually did when riding in other people's Range Rovers.

"Yup," she replied, "Among a million other things I had done to it."

"I see," I said, looking around, "It's cute."

"What's your address?" she asked, her hand extended, fingertips on the touch screen radio.

I recited my address to her as she punched the information into her navigation. Then we sat back and rode away from the busy Los Angeles airport.

Between Leslie singing along to the radio and making a million calls to let the world know she was back in town, she and I didn't talk at all during the thirty-five minute ride to my Calabasas home. Instead, I gazed out the window the whole time. *Home Sweet Home*, I thought as I looked upon the daunting traffic, cluster of plastic people, and city of dreamers and schemers. *Home Sweet Home.*

**Lisa Wu Hartwell
and Miasha**

Sheryl

It was a dreary morning, and a Monday at that, so most people in the waiting area of the Department of Family and Children Services appeared like they didn't want to be bothered.

That made me nervous, but Ramona -- who was with me -- kept reminding me that everything would be all right. Her predictions didn't help me any, though. In fact, her being there made me more nervous. I was afraid that I would be told something I didn't want to hear and have an episode in front of her. Although she knew what I had been going through over the past few months, I never liked for her or anyone for that matter to see me cry or appear emotionally unstable. But she insisted she accompany me so I gave in.

"Hi, I have an appointment with Mrs. Ruth Kyle," I said as I approached the sign-in desk.

"WHO?" the graying, forty-something-year-old woman asked in an obnoxious tone.

I looked down at my phone, which had the appointment details in its calendar. I read the name as I saw it, "Ruth Kyle," I repeated.

"Oh, Mrs. Kyle," she said. "Here sign in." She handed me a clipboard with a sheet filled halfway with names and signatures.

I wrote in my information and Ramona and I took a seat. Looking around I felt like the odd ball. Everyone appeared to be destitute, poverty-stricken, and beat up by life. I felt sorry for them as I realized that the only difference between myself and most of them was that I had some money. Other than that, I was probably in the same boat as them emotionally and mentally, or maybe even worse. And who knew? If it weren't for the financial advantages I had over them I would probably blend right in. I took a few minutes to thank God for where I was and what I had.

"Mrs. Lee," my name was called in the middle of my silent prayer.

I stood up quickly and walked to the sign-in desk. Another woman, other than the front-desk lady who had signed me in, was standing behind the counter with a file in her hand.

"Yes?"

"I see that you're here to discuss Shannon Stewart."

I nodded. "Yes." I wondered what was coming next, and from the feeling I got in my gut it wasn't something good.

"You're not listed as the child's mother in our records and so therefore we are not permitted to discuss anything concerning her with you."

The words were like daggers cutting into my chest. How dare he not list me as the mother of my child? Since three days after she was born I was her mother. I was the one who bathed her, fed her, got up in the middle of the night with her, took her to every doctor's appointment, emergency room visit, school trip, extra-curricular activity, everything! He didn't do a damn thing!

I had all this in my head but no words came out my mouth. Ramona, obviously sensing something was wrong, came to my aide.

"What's the problem?" she asked.

"Nothing," I broke my silence. "There's some mistake," I tried to prevent Ramona from finding out

129

the truth about my situation, which I had hidden for the past nine years.

"I was telling Mrs. Lee that she has to be a parent to discuss anything concerning the child," the woman reiterated.

"Thank you. You've said enough." I pulled at Ramona's arm to leave.

"No, wait a minute!" Ramona resisted. "That has to be a mistake. This *is* her mother!" she protested.

"We don't have her name in our records," the woman said.

"Just come on, Ramona," I said. "He must have done something slick." I tried covering it up.

"If you can provide us with the child's birth certificate with your name on it, along with your ID, Social Security Card, and your own birth certificate, then we can look into it."

"Okay, yes that's what we'll do! We'll be right back with that!" Ramona snapped. "You have all that at the house right?" she turned to me.

My head started to spin as I realized that I never had a birth certificate for my daughter. Kenneth always kept those sorts of things in his safe. And the thought of me not ever being able to see her again because of that overcame me, throwing me into a rage.

"Listen here," I told the woman. "I promise you I'm her mother! If you go get her right now and bring her out here she will tell you herself! I don't have the paperwork because when I left my husband he took everything and denied me access to my stuff. And I'm sure it was his doing putting someone else's name on your records as the mother. But the bottom line is I did everything for that girl! I would give my life for her! And all I want to do is see her! I'm not asking to walk out here with her! I just want to see her face! That's all. And I'm telling you if you get her she will justify everything that I'm saying! Just go and get her please!"

"I'm sorry, Mrs. Lee, but it doesn't work that way. She's not kept here. She's placed in a foster home. Even if you were listed as her mother and were able to speak with someone today you wouldn't have been able to see her. Your social worker would have had to make arrangements with her foster parents for you to see her. So, why don't you go get in touch with your husband and try to get a hold of those documents. And once you get them come back and see us and we can help you locate your daughter," she said.

"You have no idea how difficult that's going to be!" I was feeling discouraged.

Ramona stepped in, "What about the fact that just a few months back she was fighting for custody of Shannon. Don't you think if she wasn't her mother the judge and the attorneys would have mentioned that then? I mean, that's a huge discrepancy."

That was a good point. I mean why didn't anyone say anything then? I rubbed my palms down my face in frustration. There had to be something I could do. I was trying to think of what but kept coming up blank.

"Okay," I took a deep breath. "Is there a supervisor or somebody I can talk to about this in private?"

"I can get my supervisor but she won't be able to talk to you about Shannon Stewart in public or in private. You have to be the child's biological mother or legal guardian." She glanced at the file, "And we don't have you listed for either one."

"Well, who the hell is listed?" Ramona asked.

"I can't give that information."

"Can you at least tell us if there's more than one person?" she probed.

"I'm sorry. I cannot give out any information whatsoever."

On that note, I decided there was nothing left for me to do but to go talk to Kenneth. It was about time I confront his ass anyway. And with the anger built up in me added to the anguish this news has brought me; I was in the perfect condition to address him. I wasn't scared or timid. I was ready and willing. I didn't care anymore. He had already taken everything from me, so what else could he do to me? Nothing. Therefore, I didn't have anything to lose.

"Let's go, Ramona. I'll have to talk this out with Kenneth."

Ramona reluctantly followed me out the building. "That's crazy that someone can get away with something like that," she complained. "What are you going to do?"

"I'm going to visit him," I told her, rushing to the car.

"At the jail?"

"That's where he is."

"You sure you wanna face him?"

"I have to. I don't have a choice."

"Can't you just get a copy of the birth certificate?"

"If I could, I would. But I can't. And soon enough you'll know why. Right now my only focus is on finding out whose name is on those records."

I took my keys from my Yves Saint Laurent pocketbook. I unlocked my car door from the keypad. I got in, started the engine and stomped on the gas.

I had one place in mind to go -- the L.A.'s Sheriff Department's Twin Towers Correctional Facility.

Leslie

C ome'ere rude boy, boy can you get it up, come'ere rude boy, boy, is you big enough . . . my ring tone sounded. Keeping one hand on the steering wheel I reached over to the passenger seat and fiddled around in my teal Hermes Pocketbook until my phone was in my palm.

"I'm on my way, grandma," I said as soon as I answered the call.

"Where the hell are you, Les? We're gonna miss the damn visit!" my grandmother's raspy Italian-accented voice pierced through my phone.

"Grandma, there's traffic. What do you want me to do, run people off the road?"

"If it'll get you here any faster! My God, Les, you landed hours ago! You know we only get two hours on Mondays!"

"I know! But what the hell? I'm driving as fast as I can. If I start speeding I'll get pulled over and we'll really miss the visit!"

"At the rate you're going you might as well take the risk!"

"Grandma, you're probably not even ready! Did you put your wig on?"

"My wig is on!"

"Are your teeth in your mouth?"

"Go to hell, Leslie!"

"Meet me there, grandma!" I hung up. "Ugh!" My grandmother knew how to get under my skin. She didn't act that way toward my sister and brother. Only me. Why she felt the need to verbally abuse me my whole life I didn't know. But she had the right one for it 'cause grandmother or no grandmother I got right back with her ass.

I was rushing to get to her house and pick her up so that we could go see my brother. Taking Angie home put me behind schedule. But it wasn't as bad as my grandma made it seem. I was only like twenty minutes behind. I just needed to get off of I-10 and I would be fine.

I exited at Robertson Boulevard toward Culver City, stayed straight on Exposition Boulevard, made a left and then a right to be on S. Robertson. I took a left at National Boulevard and from the top of the street I could see my grandmother sitting in her wheelchair out in front of her house. The expression of the Wicked Witch on her face, she rolled down the driveway ramp that she had paved for her two years ago after she had lost both feet to diabetes.

I parked at the foot of her driveway and hopped out to help her get from her chair to the passenger seat.

"Why on earth did you come in this big thing?" she grumbled. "How are you going to lift me up that high?"

"Hello, to you too, grandma," I said, opening the passenger door.

"I wasn't talking about that kind of hi," she said.

It took everything in me to bite my tongue as I folded my grandmother's wheelchair and put it in my trunk. I wanted so bad to throw the damn thing through her window and tell her to find her own way to Twin Towers.

I jumped in the driver's seat and proceeded down her block. "Put your seatbelt on, grandma. Wouldn't want you to go flyin' through the windshield if, heaven forbid, we get into an accident," I had my way of getting even.

"Kill me, bitch," my grandmother griped. "I took you out my will a long time ago."

Angie

"911. What's your emergency?" the operator answered on the first ring.

"Hi, I called about twenty minutes ago about a vandalism at my property!" I was distraught. "And no one has come yet!"

"We've sent an officer out, ma'am. He should be there any minute," she said.

I stood in my foyer peeping out the glass door. I didn't see a police car in sight.

"Any minute? You said that when I called twenty minutes ago! I am in danger! I need someone here now! I'm afraid to be in my house! I'm afraid to leave my house! I had a stalker before who broke into my home and tried to kill me! And now I come home from vacation and my car windows are busted out! I don't feel safe! Now, you need to get on the dispatch thing and tell whoever you got comin' out here to hurry up!" I was on the brink of panicking.

"Ma'am, calm down, I'm telling you. He's on his way to you right now. If it helps any, I can stay on the phone with you until he gets there."

A car pulled up to my gate. I looked into the monitor to get a close up. It was Bobby Fuller, the first person who came to mind to call the minute I noticed the damage to my car. "That won't be necessary," I told the operator. "Just please tell them to hurry!" I hung up and buzzed Bobby in.

Despite me standing Bobby up at the altar, we remained friends. He understood my position. In fact, he admitted to me that he thought we were moving too fast as well. He felt the same pressure from the networks that I felt but went along with the whole wedding for the sake of his job. At the end of the day, though, we were both on the same page; and he was thankful I had the guts to say something before it was too late.

Now we were friends although we couldn't reveal that to the world. It was to Bobby's benefit that the media and fans believed we were archenemies. If they knew Bobby was still cool with me it would impact his image. They needed to believe that I ruined his life. They needed a villain and a victim in order to sell their story. And as fucked up as it was, I respected it. It was the business.

"Oh my God, I'm so glad you're here!" I collapsed in Bobby's arms.

He hugged me back as he looked over both our shoulders.

"Come in, come in," I said, pulling him to the front door.

"What happened?" he asked, as soon as he got inside my house.

"I got home from my trip and my garage door was up. And at first I just thought that I had forgotten to close it because I was in a rush when I left, but when I walked inside I realized my car windows were shattered. I freaked out!" I explained.

"Did you call the police?"

"Yeah. They were on their way thirty minutes ago," I complained.

"Who would do that? Who would even have access? I mean, after the first incident, you tightened your security up quite a bit, right?"

"Yes! That's why I'm extra scared," I told him. "How did they get past all that high tech shit I had put in? I spent a ton of money on that security system! Matter fact, let me get them on the phone," I said, going toward the kitchen.

"You mind if I take a look?" Bobby asked as he walked toward the garage.

"You're not scared?"

"I'm a man," he said, ego flaring.

"O-kay," I said. "Do you. Just please holler out to me if you see somebody. Don't be like they be in the horror flicks and go all quiet on me. Warn me, shit." I teased as I looked through the Rolodex sitting on the built-in desk in my kitchen.

I flipped through the cards, looking for the security company who had supposedly installed the best of the best alarm systems, video monitoring, and deterrent devices on the market. So much for that shit. Somebody owed me an explanation and a refund!

"ANGIE!" Bobby called out to me.

On full alert, I answered, "HUH?"

"HAVE YOU BEEN IN HERE?"

"NO! WELL, I MEAN, I WENT TO THE GARAGE DOOR AND SOON AS I SAW MY BACK WINDSHIELD BUSTED I RAN THE OTHER WAY!"

"YOU NEED TO COME HERE AND SEE THIS!"

I hurried to the garage anxious to see what Bobby discovered, hoping it wasn't more damage.

"What is it?" I asked from the top of the garage stairs.

"Come here," he said.

I walked down the stairs.

"Look," he was standing in front of my car.

I saved your life, bitch was spray painted on the hood of my Porsche.

Sheryl

"Sheryl, are you sure you want to go through with this?" Ramona asked as I pulled up to the front of her house to drop her off.

Without looking at her I responded, "It's all I can do, Ramona."

"Can't you get his mom or his sister or somebody else to go talk to him and find out the information?"

"His mom hated me the minute I married him and tapped into her spending money, as she so eloquently put it, at our wedding reception. And his sister doesn't know the real story so she wouldn't help. This is something only him and I can discuss," I finally made eye contact with Ramona.

"I just don't think it's a good idea, Sheryl. To go see him after all he's --"

I cut Ramona off before she got the chance to talk me out of doing what was necessary. "Remember that night when I left Kenneth for good and came to your house?"

"Yeah."

"And you asked me what made me stay that long?"

Ramona nodded.

"And I said for my child? And then you said, 'Well I guess when it comes to your child you gotta do what you gotta do?"

"Um hum." Ramona remembered clearly.

"Well here we go again," I said simply.

Ramona said no more. She opened the passenger door and stepped out. "I'm here if you need me," she said, probably realizing that that was all she could do was be there for me.

**Lisa Wu Hartwell
and Miasha**

Leslie

We pulled up to Bauchet Street at eleven fifty. Visiting hours ended at twelve forty-five and didn't start up again until two-thirty. There was no way in hell I was going to be stuck waiting around with my grandma for two and a half hours so I rushed into a parking space and prayed we could make the visit before it ended.

Upon entering the correctional facility my grandma and me had to show our IDs. We were then instructed to secure all our belongings with the exception of our locker key and ID cards. From there we were searched thoroughly. They even lifted my grandmother out of her wheelchair and turned it upside down looking for weapons or contraband of any kind. Finally, a deputy summoned us and escorted us to the visiting floor.

By the time we got up there and came face to face with my brother, it was twelve fifteen. We only had thirty minutes to spend with him and he was upset.

"What the hell, man?" he barked as soon as he sat down. "Hi grandma," he leaned over and kissed our grandmother on both cheeks.

"How are you?" she asked.

He sighed, "Hanging in there, I guess," he said. His pale skin looked like it was glued to his bones. There was no meat between the two whatsoever. His bright green eyes bulged like they were too big for his face. And his dirty-blonde hair seemed to be thinning.

Between drugs and jail my once good-looking, well-kept brother had turned into an aging skeleton.

"Why are you guys so late?" he asked, looking at me.

"You know I was on a trip for my therapy sessions," I reminded him.

"It was a vacation," my grandmother butted in. "Then she dropped someone off like that was part of the plan," she added.

My brother shook his head then got to the point of our visit. "Well, anyway, I'm just glad you guys are here." He turned to me. "Listen, I'm gonna need you to do me a big favor, sis."

I exhaled, "What?"

"I need you to go to her house," he said. "Tell that lady the situation. The real deal so she can drop the fuckin' charges. That's the only way I have a chance. Unless you guys can come up with lawyer money. Otherwise I'm goin' to die in here." He put the guilt trip on us.

"Don't talk like that, Danny," my grandmother commanded. "We're gonna get you outta here. You don't need to be in here. Look at you. You're getting so skinny, it's scary. What are they feeding you in here, birdseeds? Look at you. I'm worried sick about you," she went on.

"It's crazy, I know, grandma. That's why I need to get out of this fuckin' place. Leslie, I need you to go to her house and tell her I was set up. That crazy bitch said she was going to pay me five hundred dollars. All I was supposed to do was go in there with her, hide out, chase the chick around a little, and then she was supposed to come and scare me off. I was going to get my money and go get so fuckin' high I would forget the shit ever happened --"

"Danny," my grandmother shook her head in disgust, "Don't talk that drug shit in front of me."

My brother paid her no mind as he continued, "But next thing I know I'm bleeding from my head and being arrested. That psycho bitch set me up!"

"Who are you talking about?" I asked my brother. "What psycho bitch?"

"I don't know her name. She came through skid row offering money. I was desperate you know. I just remember the address. I need you to go there and tell the woman my story. Beg her to drop the charges before my trial. It's the only way I'll get outta here."

"Why can't you just tell your side of the story on the stand?" I asked. "I mean, if it's true it'll add up right?"

"They'll never believe me, a fuckin' stone-head. Come on. Are you kidding me?"

"Stop saying that," my grandmother interjected. "You're no stone-head. You're my grandson. You just caught a raw deal." She glanced at me. "I just wish you'd get it together."

"Grandma, don't start okay," my brother said. "Don't start with the mushy shit."

"I can't help it," my grandmother was starting to cry. "You were such a good kid, on the right track before that . . ." my grandmother lowered her head as she wiped her eyes with her hand.

"All right, enough!" my brother said. "I can't take this shit."

I looked at my watch as I sucked up the tears I felt gathering in my eyes. "We only have ten minutes left. Can we talk about something positive please?"

"Here," my brother slyly slid me a piece of paper. "Go there. Please."

144

I glanced down at the paper. "1849 Cold Canyon Road," I mumbled, "This address is so familiar."

And right before I realized whose address it was I was distracted by some commotion coming from the other side of the visiting area.

Angie

I had called the police back and told them not to bother coming. I lied and said that after taking a second look I saw that a baseball had been thrown through my window and that there was an apology note on my door from my neighbor so I would take the damage up with her.

I thanked Bobby for coming to my rescue and apologized for having him come for nothing. Of course, being the perfect gentleman that he was, he said it was not a problem and that if I ever needed him again not to hesitate calling. I saw him to the door and watched him pull out of my driveway and through my gates. Then I immediately called Deidre.

"Why would you do that?!" I screamed into the phone as soon as she said hello. "I called the police and everything! They would've arrested you! Then what?"

"Then maybe once I was gone you would've realized what you had!" Deidre retorted.

I was heated. This whole situation with her had gotten way out of control. "Are you serious?" I was baffled. "How did we get to this? We were good friends," I pled. "Now we're going at each other's throats every time I turn around. Why did it come to this?"

"I went out of my way for you, Angie! To show you that I loved you and that I wanted to be with you and you turned around and discarded me like trash! Now I feel like I have to do things like this to get your attention! Otherwise, you act like I never existed to you!"

"You know what, Deidre? This is just over my head. I never knew we were serious. I mean, you introduced me to a new side of myself, yeah, but after that I thought I made it clear that we would remain friends."

"And that was fine with me! Until you wanted to have a bunch more friends!" she argued.

"But I'm entitled to," I defended myself. "I'm a single woman."

"Well, I thought I could change that," she stated. "I thought that I could change everything! That I could create the life I had dreamt for so many years. I thought I could make it my reality. And I had the perfect plan, too. Then in an instant it backfired. And I was left in the cold," she explained.

I waited patiently for Deidre to finish pouring out her wishful thoughts. Then I decided that instead of continue to argue with her I would give her some words of wisdom and hope that I could civilly end our friendship gone awry.

"Deidre, had I known you were going to try to change me into someone you wanted me to be, I would have never crossed the line of friendship with you. My mother told me a long time ago, you can never add ingredients to a cake that's already made."

I thought about my mother, a strong-willed, adventurous, independent woman until after she married my father. He preferred a housewife, and although she conformed she wasn't happy. She spent twenty years dedicating every second of her life to my father, me, and our home. Then she got sick and it was on her deathbed that she joked it wasn't cancer that was killing her, but boredom. She told me to never let a man change who I was and provided me with the analogy about a cake.

"But --" Deidre's cracking voice interrupted my thoughts.

"Let's just call a truce," I said, realizing that Deidre and I would never work. She was exactly the type of person my mother had warned me to stay away from. "No hard feelings," I told her. "No love lost. Let's both take this as a huge learning experience and walk away while we each still have some dignity left."

There was a brief pause. Then, "Fair enough," Deidre said softly.

"Good bye, Deidre."

"Bye."

Sheryl

"**W**HO IS SHE?" I was sick of playing games with Kenneth. He'd been taunting me since I got there in the visiting area.

With a devilish grin, he questioned, "Is that the real reason you came up here? Or did you start missing me?"

"I WOULDN'T MISS YOU IF YOU FELL OFF THE FACE OF THIS EARTH! NOW TELL ME WHOSE NAME YOU PUT DOWN AS SHANNON'S MOTHER AND YOU CAN GO BACK TO BENDING OVER LIKE THE BITCH THAT YOU ARE!" I shouted, with a look in my eyes that I wish could really kill.

"Hahahahaha," he laughed. "It's funny the heart you get around maximum security. Had you tried this shit back home, I would had put my foot so far up ya ass you woulda been cummin' shoestrings! You fuckin' whore!"

"Sheryl?" a very familiar voice intervened.

I turned around to see Leslie standing over my shoulder.

"Well I'll be damned, speak of the devil," Kenneth said, staring at Leslie like she was a ghost.

"Kenneth?" Leslie looked back and forth at Kenneth and me with a puzzled look on her face.

"You know him?" I asked her.

"Oh yeah," Kenneth answered for her. "And I guess it's 'bout time you get to know her too."

I looked at Leslie. She was staring at Kenneth. I looked at him. His face was covered with satisfaction as he seemingly forced his eyes off Leslie and turned to me.

"Hers," he said.

"Hers what?"

"You wanted to know whose name I put down as Shannon's mother didn't you?"

I heard him but I didn't believe him. I couldn't. There was no way. I just spent a weekend with this woman and considered her a friend. There was no way she could be the same woman who my husband had a baby by to cover up the fact that I couldn't conceive.

Leslie stood frozen. She seemed as surprised as me. But how could she have been? She was the one who made the fuckin' deal to sell her baby. And now that I thought about it, she excused herself at the dress burning ceremony when she heard me tell my story like it was too much for her to handle. But she probably never expected that I'd turn out to be the wife of the motherfucker she sold her baby to. I bet that was too much to take in that night. Without doing much more thinking I felt myself lose control as my hands rose up and landed around Leslie's neck. It was as if I was having an outer body experience. I could see myself choking this woman but I couldn't stop myself.

Kenneth's evil laugh played in my mind like a soundtrack. Screams and shouts from other visitors and the guards were heard in slow motion. The world seemed to have stopped spinning as I felt myself being forcefully pulled away from a choking Leslie.

Coughing and crying simultaneously, Leslie looked like she wanted to say something but I was glad she was unable to. Hearing her voice, knowing that she was the one who had ultimately taken away my womanhood, would have thrown me into a rage. All these years I lived with the fact that some woman out there had the audacity to agree to sleep with my husband, have his child for me to raise, and walk away like it was nothing more than a favor. I always wondered what kind of woman could do something like that. And I always told myself that if I ever found out I would wring her fuckin' neck.

Leslie

I walked out of the prison in shambles. An officer had to push my grandma because my hands were trembling too much for me to do it. The minute we walked through the doors to the outside, I lit a cigarette.

"Why didn't you press charges when the cop asked if that's what you wanted to do, Les? That woman was tryin' to kill you!" my grandmother asked, fury outlining the wrinkles on her face.

I stopped walking and held my lighter to the tip of my cigarette with one hand and cuffed the flame with the other. Taking a long puff and then exhaling, I looked at the officer then at my grandma, my eyes squinted from the sun, I said, "I don't want to talk about it right now."

"Who was she?"

Another puff and I answered, "I don't want to talk about it."

"How do you even know her?"

"Grandma!"

"Ma'am, do you need me to walk you two to your vehicle?" the officer jumped in.

I shook my head, meanwhile my grandma was saying yes.

"Is that a yes or a no?" The officer was clearly sick of us.

I took a final puff of the cigarette and jammed it between the officer's fingers. "Can you trash that for me?" I asked, grabbing hold of my grandmother's wheelchair.

He had a disgusted look on his face as he stood there stiff holding my half smoked cigarette.

I pushed my grandmother to the car, trying hard to control my jitters. But the more I tried not to think about what had just happened the more my mind seemed to wander to it.

"What are you doing?" I asked Kenneth as he swaddled our new baby girl.

He didn't answer me. He just proceeded getting our baby ready for the outside.

I repeated myself, louder, "WHAT ARE YOU DOING?"

No reply. It was as if he couldn't hear me. Like I was invisible even. I got up to get in his face and make myself visible and I couldn't feel my legs. I bent down to touch my knees to make sure they were still there. I felt them with my hands but I couldn't feel them to make them move.

"Kenneth, what's happening to me?" I asked. "I can't walk!" I was panicking.

Kenneth continued to ignore me. He grabbed some bottles out the fridge and put them in the diaper bag that was on my sofa.

"KENNETH! ARE YOU LISTENING TO ME? SOMETHING'S WRONG! I CAN'T FEEL MY LEGS!" I screamed to the top of my lungs.

He glanced up at me and I felt a quick moment of relief as I figured he did see me. I wasn't losing my mind. I wasn't invisible. "KENNETH, I NEED HELP!"

Kenneth walked toward me, our baby in his arms and diaper bag over his shoulder. He knelt down to meet me eye-to-eye.

"Listen to me," he said. "I'm going to take her and give her the life she deserves. And as for you, you're going to go on about your life like this never happened."

"What?" I was completely confused. It was at that point that I thought I was dreaming. Like what was happening wasn't real.

"If this ever gets back to my wife, your legs won't be the only things to stop working."

My brain seemed to register the information at a slower pace than my body as I was trying with all my might to leap on Kenneth as he turned to walk away. I felt the upper part of my body lunge forward but the bottom half crippled me. I just fell to the floor.

As Kenneth got to my front door, I started trying to crawl to him. I was screaming and crying as I realized it was not a joke. Kenneth was seriously kidnapping my three-day old child.

My pleading didn't do me any justice. That's when I went for the phone. I dialed the police. They came out to my apartment and I filed a report. They took the descriptions of Kenneth and my baby girl and asked if I had any other information like an address or telephone number. I was devastated when I couldn't tell them anything. I had no information on Kenneth other than his first and last name.

I shamefully explained to the police that Kenneth was married and therefore never gave me any of his personal information. I had only known him for a few weeks before I got pregnant. And during my pregnancy he only came around for doctor's appointments and the birth. It was my understanding that I was going to raise my child alone and only get financial support from her father. I had no idea he would steal her from me.

The police said they would start an investigation but demanded I take a drug test after I told them that I couldn't stop Kenneth because my legs had gone completely numb. I didn't care. I was drug free so it didn't matter. If that would get them to start tracking down my daughter any faster than I'd take one in a heartbeat.

The problem was it came back positive for PSD, an illegal hallucinogen. It was obviously slipped to me by Kenneth. But the police were not trying to hear that. When they finally caught up with Kenneth, he made it seem like I was a drug addict and agreed to let him take care of our child until I got my life in order. Since it was his word against mine, we had to go to court.

Before the first court date, I got threats on my life. One night I even woke up to a Molotov cocktail crashing through my living room window. None of it backed me down. It actually made me want to fight harder. But when I got a picture of my little girl with a plastic bag over her face and a letter attached threatening to kill her if I came to court, that did it. I took the photo to the police.

After close examination, they pointed out that it was a doll dressed in a baby's clothing and further concluded, with the help of Kenneth's team of high-powered attorneys, that I had taken the photo and doctored the letter to make it seem like it came from Kenneth. I looked like the crazy drug addict Kenneth made me out to be.

I didn't show up to court; not because I had given up fighting for my daughter, but because I knew I had no chance of winning. I hadn't had the right defense team. And the positive drug test and photo of the doll made me look bad. I told myself I would wait to fight the case when I could afford a team of lawyers. I gave *myself six months. But the truth of the matter was, six months was not enough time to come up with the type of money I needed to go against Kenneth. And the more time went by the more scared I was to even go through with it.*

I started believing that maybe my baby was better off with Kenneth and his wife, in a financially secure two-parent household. I started doubting myself, doubting whether or not I could even be a good mother. And before long, six months turned to six years. And I had done my best to put the whole situation out of my head -- through indulging in men, sex and money.

I put my grandmother in the car, her wheelchair in the trunk, started the engine and rolled the windows down. I was pacing by the driver's door, smoking a cigarette, when my cell phone rang.

"Hello," I answered without even looking to see who it was.

"What the fuck, dude?" my brother whined in the phone.

I pulled my cell away from my ear and looked at the screen. He was calling me from an unblocked number and it wasn't collect like usual.

"Danny, whose phone are you calling me from?"

"My cellmate's. But that's not important. What the hell happened? Who was that chick? And why did you leave grandma and me abruptly like that to go over there and say something to her in the first place? Now they're talking about removing you from my visitor's list!" he fussed.

"Danny, since you're not calling me from the prison phone, this call isn't being recorded is it?" I asked, bypassing everything my brother was just yelling about.

"Why does it matter?"

"Just answer the question, Danny."

"No. It's not being recorded. It's a cell phone. They don't even know he has it in here."

"I need you to do me a favor," I puffed the cigarette.

"What can I do for you from in here, Leslie? Besides, right now I'm the one who needs the help."

"What if I can promise to get you out of there?"

"How so?"

"I know why that address you gave me sounds familiar. And I know who lives there. I can get her to drop the charges before your trial. I just need you to take care of something for me before you get out."

"What?"

"That inmate, who the girl who choked me was talking to, his name is Kenneth Stewart."

"Yeah, what about 'im?"

"He's the guy, Danny." Tears escaped my eyes. Wiping them with the back of my shaking hand, I elaborated, "He's the guy who took my baby."

"I'll kill 'im dead," my brother declared.

"Do it, Danny, and I will get you out of there," I made a deal with my brother.

My grandma looked at me. Her hard life depicted in her cold eyes. "I always said you were your father's child," she muffled.

That's when it hit me why my grandmother hated me. She viewed me as my father. *That bitch*, I thought as I put my cigarette out. How dare she put me in the same category as that monster? He killed my mother in front of Danny and me just because she poured out the alcohol that was causing him to beat on her. I wanted Kenneth dead because he stole my child from me. There was a got damn difference!

Angie

After I hung up with Deidre I called my insurance company. They had me on hold forever, then when somebody finally came to the phone they wound up having to transfer me. That was another lengthy hold. Meanwhile, I put the phone on speaker and started unpacking my clothes.

"Hello, thanks for holding, how can I help you?" a woman's voice spoke.

I hurriedly retrieved my phone off my bed. I took it off speaker and put it to my ear.

"Hello, yes, I would like to set up a claim."

"Can I have your policy number?"

I read the woman the ten-digit number on the front of my insurance card.

"Okay, can you verify your name and address?"

"Angela Barnes. 1849 Cold Canyon Road, Calabasas California, 91302."

"Okay, please hold while I pull up your policy."

At that, my other line started beeping. I looked to see who it was. It was Leslie. I didn't want to click over and risk losing my connection with the insurance company. I had spent too much time on hold for that. So I pressed the ignore button and continued holding for the customer service rep to pull up my policy.

Sheryl

"Hey, lady, get out the got damn fast lane!" an older white guy shouted at me as he passed me on my right.

Horns were blowing behind me like I was leading a parade. In my rear view mirror I could see the traffic build-up I had caused. Typically under the circumstances where I'd be crying until I was visionless and emotionally too unstable to concentrate on the task of driving, I would just pull over on the shoulder or get off the highway until I gathered my composure enough to drive regularly again. But, for some reason that day, my mind wasn't even powerful enough to convince me to get off the road.

I completely lost every bit of sense I had. I was murmuring crazy thoughts that in the past I had been able to suppress. And this time I was highly considering acting on them. I switched lanes finally to the relief of the motorists in the left lane but to the dismay of the ones in the right. The horn blowing followed me as I haphazardly swerved into place.

"You're gonna kill somebody!" a female driver angrily warned.

Hoping that somebody would be me I ignored her as I did all the other grumbles, middle fingers, and callous stares. I stayed the course. Driving straight non-stop, as I had been doing for at least the past hour headed to my final destination.

**Lisa Wu Hartwell
and Miasha**

Leslie

"Come on pick up the phone," I prayed. "Pick up, Angie." I was sitting behind the wheel in my grandmother's driveway. I had dropped her off and was trying to get a hold of Angie, but her cell phone kept forwarding me to her voicemail. I didn't want to leave a message. I needed to speak with her.

I ended the call after again being sent to voicemail and as I was getting ready to redial, I had an incoming call from Angie. I pushed the green phone icon instantly.

"Angie!"

"What's going on?" her voice carried a tone of concern.

"I need to come to your house and talk to you about some very important things. And in the meantime, I need you to give me Sheryl's number," I spoke rushed and with urgency.

"O-kay," she hesitated. "But what's the matter?"

"It's a long story. I'll tell it to you when I get to your house. Do you still have that note Sheryl wrote you with her number on it? Mine blew away."

"Yeah. It's in my pocketbook. Hold on."

I was backing out of my grandmother's driveway as I held for Sheryl's number. Once onto the street, I shifted the car to drive and started down my grandmother's well-maintained street.

160

"Hello," Angie returned to the phone. "It's 323 . . ." she started.

"You know what? Can you just call her on the three-way for me? I'm driving. I won't be able to take it down."

"Okay, hold on."

"Wait, Angie!"

"Huh?"

"Don't tell her I'm on the phone. Just merge me in."

"What is going on?" Angie needed to know.

"I'm telling you it's a long story but I promise to give you all the details when I get there. According to navigation I'm like twenty minutes from you."

"All right," she let out an unsatisfied sigh. Then she clicked over.

After a few seconds, I was rejoined with Angie.

"Leslie," Angie said.

"Hm?"

"She didn't answer."

"Oh, my God." A weird sense of emptiness came over me. "Keep trying her, Angie," I commanded. "I'll be right there."

I hung up the phone to focus on driving as fast as I could without being pulled over or getting into an accident. I needed to get to Angie's and explain the entire situation in enough time to try to reach out to Sheryl with a plan of revenge. I felt if she heard my side of the story along with my plot on how we could get that motherfucker Kenneth back, then she would be okay. Until then, there was no telling what she'd do. I mean, it was no secret she was the weakest of all the women at the Dress Burning Ceremony. And quite frankly, after learning that it was Kenneth who she had been married to for thirteen years, I could see why.

Lisa Wu Hartwell
and Miasha

He was a kind of evil that was unexplainable. I often thought of him as being inhuman. After what he had done to my child and me, I considered him the devil. And now it was time for him to go to hell where he belonged. Fuck what my grandmother or anybody else thought about it.

Sheryl

My phone was ringing back to back, and it was nobody but Angie. I guessed Leslie had told her what had happened at the prison. I was in no mood to discuss it so I ignored the calls. However, when Ramona called I decided to answer and only because I didn't want her to worry about me. That would cause her to involve too many of my family members. I didn't want them to know all of what was going on. I never wanted to burden them with my issues. Especially since I was not their blood relative. I went my whole life trying to stay out of their way and off their backs. I was just grateful they had adopted me. Anything else would have been asking for too much, in my opinion. And for that reason I never ever bothered them with any of my problems.

"Hello," I answered, as calmly as I could.

"Sheryl, are you okay?" Ramona asked. "It's going on three o'clock. Visiting hours at the jail were over at twelve forty-five," Ramona said.

I wanted to ask her how she knew that, and wondered why she'd even looked up that information. Why was she keeping tabs on me? But to get her off the phone quickly I had to make her feel as comfortable as possible in the notion that I was okay.

"I know. I just decided to take a drive afterward. Clear my mind. I'll be home soon. The traffic is starting to pick up so it may take me a little longer than expected, though," I managed to come up with.

"Well, who's Angie?" she threw a monkey wrench in the plan.

"Who?"

"Angie. She called here asking that I call you and check on you. She said she got the house number from Dr. Anna --"

A huge monkey wrench, I thought as I jumped to the question of why Dr. Anna would go against her privacy policy and give my home number out.

"That's breaking the law," I said. "Dr. Anna has no right giving out any information about me to anybody."

"Exactly," Ramona agreed. "And that's when I figured there must be something very wrong if she was that concerned to go to the length of risking her practice."

"Oh God, what now?" I gasped as my car started to stall to a halt.

"What's wrong, Sheryl?"

I looked at the dashboard. My gaslight was on, for how long I didn't know. I hadn't paid any attention to it since I had left the prison.

URRRRRK BOOM!

In a flash my car was smacked from behind. My body lifted and jerked forward with so much force my head smashed the front windshield. My seatbelt kept me from being ejected from the car as it caught my body and slung it backward. My head bounced off the headrest and fell forward onto the airbag, which had burst through the steering wheel. A burning sensation covered my entire face at the impact. I heard screams and breaks screeching, horns and glass shattering. I could even hear Ramona yelling my name through the phone. But I couldn't respond. I couldn't even call for help. I was trapped, unable to move a single muscle.

164

I closed my eyes and tried to block out the sounds around me. Prepared to die, I figured it was my fate. Clearly my intention was to go to San Francisco to the Golden Gate Bridge and jump off. But apparently I didn't have enough gas for that. However, God still granted me my wish. And it was then I truly learned the meaning of *be careful what you wish for*.

Leslie

I pulled up to Angie's gated home. She buzzed me in and I drove up to the front of her house. She met me at the door. I turned off the engine, reached in the backseat to grab my pocketbook and jumped out the car. I followed her inside her estate home.

A million thoughts running through my mind, I couldn't comment on the lavish décor but indeed it was hard not to notice.

"So what in the world is going on, Leslie?" Angie asked, leading me to her chef's kitchen.

She took a glass of wine from the counter and placed it on the Horchow banquette table in front of the spot she invited me to sit.

I wasted no time sipping it. I needed something to calm me down.

"Okay, where do I start?" I was frazzled.

"At the beginning," Angie stated the obvious.

"Right," I said. Reaching in my pocketbook, I landed my hand on my pack of cigarettes. "You mind if I smoke?"

Angie shook her head, hopped off the barstool, and walked over to the bay windows in her breakfast nook. She opened them.

"So, I went to the prison to see my brother today --"

"You got a brother in prison?" Angie stopped me.

"I didn't tell you in Tahiti?"

"No!"

"Oh, where were you when I told Sheryl?"

"I must've been making drinks."

"That's right. You were."

"But anyway," Angie said, "finish talking. I didn't mean to cut you off."

"Okay, so I'm at the prison visiting my brother and it's some shit behind that, too, but I'll get to that after I tell you about Sheryl." My brain was scrambled. "I hear a woman get loud in the visiting room. So I look up and it's Sheryl. I go over to see what's going on and I notice that the guy she's visiting is this guy I used to date. And actually I had a baby by him, which is the same child Sheryl was there at the prison asking him about --"

"What the hell --" Angie was completely in shock.

"It's a twisted ass mess, I know." I puffed my cigarette. "I still can't believe it. And now that I think back, those ultrasound pictures she had at the dress burning ceremony were mine. That son of a bitch made it seem like he was just that excited about having a baby. I didn't know he was using those to help his wife fake a fuckin' pregnancy!"

Angie's eyes grew ten times their size, "Oh my God, you're not the woman who basically sold her baby to Sheryl's husband are you?"

"I never sold my baby," I said quickly, trying to make the situation clear. "And that's why it didn't dawn on me at the ceremony that I was the woman she was talking about."

"Then, why did you get up and leave?" Angie asked.

"Because I know how it is to lose a child to a man just because he's more powerful than you." I grew emotional as I pointed my finger at Angie, "That motherfucker drugged me and kidnapped my child! Then made it impossible for me to get her back!" I puffed my cigarette and blew the smoke out. "I got up and left because her story brought back too many memories. I had no idea that they were my own."

Angie was about to say something but was interrupted by her phone. Looking around, trying to follow the ring, she spotted her phone on the counter near her Viking refrigerator.

She got down off the stool and went to get it. "Hello."

I couldn't hear what was being said on the other end. But from the look on Angie's face it wasn't anything good.

"Who was that?" I asked, worried.

"Sheryl's roommate. Sheryl was in an accident on I5 --"

"I5? What was she doing on I5?"

"I don't know," Angie said, closing her kitchen window. "But we need to get to Bakersfield Memorial Hospital. Wherever the hell that is."

I gulped down the wine and rushed behind Angie toward her front door.

"You gonna ride with me or follow me?" I asked, power walking over to the drivers door.

"I have to ride with you," she said, locking her door with a code. "Somebody broke the windows out of my car."

A light bulb went off in my head. I got in the car and started it. Driving through Angie's gates, I said, "That's the other thing I needed to talk to you about."

Angie looked over at me with an expression like she hoped it wasn't more bad news.

"My brother is the guy who you had arrested for stalking you," I broke the news.

"WHAT?! Daniel Caruso is your brother?!" she exclaimed.

I nodded. "But --" I needed to diffuse the situation before it could even escalate, "listen to me and hear me out. My brother didn't break into your house, and he wasn't stalking you --"

Angie objected, "I caught him! I saw him with my own eyes! My friend knocked him unconscious. He laid on my kitchen floor until the cops came to arrest him!"

"Listen," I told her, "you're right, he was there. That was him. But that friend who you said knocked him over the head, she wouldn't happen to be the same friend who busted your car windows would she?"

Angie frowned, "What does one have to do with the other?"

"Is she?"

"Yeah, she is! But, like I said, what does that have to do with your brother being in my house?"

"She let him in, Angie. She paid him to do all of that. And my brother being a strung out heroin addict, he was desperate for the money. But it was not part of their deal for him to be hit over the head and arrested. She added that shit after the fact." I glanced over at Angie to see how she was taking what I was telling her. Her face was stone. "I don't know what she was trying to prove to you, but that wasn't my brother's doing at all."

"Oh my God." Angie threw her palm over her mouth. "No she didn't."

I took that as confirmation that she believed my story. Now all I needed was for her to agree to drop all charges so my brother could be released, and in turn he could fulfill his end of our bargain.

"Does it make sense to you now?"

Angie nodded slowly. "She's crazy as hell."

"So, are you goin' to drop the charges?"

Angie smirked, still a look of utter shock on her face, "I guess, I'm going to have to."

"Okay, good. Now my brother can handle Kenneth for me."

"What do you mean handle Kenneth for you?" she looked over at me.

"I promised that I would get my brother out of jail if he would turn Kenneth into maggot food."

"You mean like, kill him?" Angie quizzed.

"Absolutely."

"Are you serious?"

Keeping my eyes on the approaching intersection I said, "Hell yeah."

"You'll go to hell for that, Leslie."

"As long as he gets there first I don't care. That man ruined my whole life. I was never the same after that day. I lost my mind. I punished myself. I did crazy things like get a hysterectomy so that I could never again experience the pain of carrying a child and having it stripped from me." I puffed the butt of my cigarette long and hard to keep back the river of tears that was forming in my eyes. "And then I started dating married men just 'cause I didn't think a non-married man would want to settle down with a woman who couldn't have children. I figured married men already had children so they wouldn't care if I could have any or not."

"This is one twisted ass man to have caused you and Sheryl the type of mental anguish he caused, I agree," Angie said, slowly. "But there's other ways to get him back that don't include risking you or your brother's freedom," she said. "Besides, killin' somebody like him would only be giving him an easy way out. People like him you want to suffer."

I threw my finished cigarette out the window. I wiped my eyes with the front and back of my palm. "What do you have in mind?"

Sheryl

I opened my eyes and was confronted with a room full of well-known faces. My mom, sister, an aunt, Ramona and even a couple of Eric's relatives were all gathered around. For a quick second I thought time had rewound itself and I was at my wedding. Just as I started to feel relieved and elated as if I had finally awoke from a nightmare, Ramona brought me back to reality.

"She's awake." Her worried eyes were on me.

Suddenly I had everybody's immediate attention. My mom approached me first, leaning over me, her eyes wandered about my face; I assumed examining the injuries I sustained in the accident it just occurred to me I had been in.

"How are you feeling?" she asked, looking me in the eyes.

"Stiff," I responded, my mouth dry and sticky like I could have been suffering from dehydration.

"Hi, Sheryl, are you okay?" my aunt asked, from the distance from which she stood.

I nodded slightly.

"You are so blessed," Eric's sister said.

"Yes, you are," my mom agreed. "From the looks of the car it's no way you should be alive," my mom said, gently using the tips of her delicate fingers to brush my hair back off my forehead.

"Make sure you thank God," my aunt added.

I was gracefully taking in the messages of care and concern, but anxiously waiting for someone to tell me what my injuries were, how long I'd be in the hospital, and how I could expect to recover.

"What happened to me?" I mumbled.

Right then an average-height Middle Eastern woman with a long braid down her back, thin-framed glasses, and broken English entered the room.

"Hello, eddiebody," she greeted the roomful.

We all returned the greeting.

She introduced herself as my nurse and then walked over to my bedside. "You're awake," she smiled.

I tried cracking one back at her.

She looked at the monitor I was hooked up to and jotted some things down in a file she was cradling between the bend in her arm. She looked up at the IV bag. "Almost empty," she said under her breath. Then fixing her eyes back on me, she asked, "Are you in any pain?"

I shook my head. "Just thirsty," I told her, desperately wanting to moisten my mouth.

"I'll get you sumpting to drink."

"I can get her something," Ramona butted in. "Can she have anything?"

The woman looked at Ramona and nodded. "Yes. She won't be gedding anymore surgeries."

"I had surgery?" I asked the woman as Ramona left the room.

The woman's face dropped a little. She glanced over at my relatives. My sister rolled her eyes and turned away. My mom's eyes welled with water. My aunt seemed to pretend like she wasn't paying my question or me any attention anymore. And Eric's sister placed her son's head in her chest, covering his ear with her hand.

My heart skipped a beat, as I had no idea what to expect the nurse's reply to be. I looked at her. Anxiety building.

"What did I have surgery for?" I questioned.

"You've sustained spinal cord injury in the crash," she said gently. "Surgery was needed to stabilize your spine."

All I heard was spinal cord injury and I tuned everything else out. The strong possibility that I would be a paraplegic consumed me.

"Well, how did it go? I mean, were the doctors able to fix it? I mean, I won't be paralyzed will I? I will be able to walk again, right?"

I looked around at everybody's reaction. My mom lowered her head into her chest. My sister walked out the room.

Without having to hear it from the nurse, I knew what the response was. Immediately I started trying to move my legs. I had to prove them wrong. I had to show the hospital personnel and my family that the prognosis was a mistake. But as hard as I tried to move below my waist, I couldn't. Not even a foot would budge. I had no feeling whatsoever in my lower body. And when that realization kicked in it killed me. Suicide mission complete, I thought. Only I was stuck to live this one out.

Angie

After driving for two hours to get to the hospital Sheryl was taken to and another hour in the wrong direction thanks to Leslie's navigation, it had taken us almost four hours to get to the emergency room.

We hurriedly parked the car in one of the available parking spaces and Leslie and I lightly jogged across the lot over to the automatic doors of the hospital. Once inside we approached the front desk.

We gave the woman Sheryl's name and the nature of her emergency and the woman looked her up in the computer.

"She's been taken to ICU," the woman informed us without taking her eyes off the computer monitor. She recited a room number to us and instructed us to go to the main entrance of the hospital to access the Intensive Care Unit.

"Oh my God, ICU?" I thought aloud as Leslie and I briskly walked back to the car.

"How bad could it have been?" Leslie asked.

We drove to the visitor's parking lot, got a ticket and parked. We took the elevator to the lobby of the hospital. At the information desk we again gave Sheryl's name but that time we had a room number as well. The guy behind the desk dressed in a security uniform directed us where to go.

We had to take yet another elevator to the fifth floor. Once there we had to stop at another desk, this one being a nurse's station.

175

"We're here to see Sheryl Lee," we said simultaneously.

"What relation to the patient are you?" she asked something no one else had asked us.

We glanced at each other. Then Leslie blurted, "We're her sisters."

The woman looked at Leslie suspiciously prompting Leslie to clarify.

"We were all adopted," she said.

The woman nodded her head, "Oh okay," she said. "I'll have to call back there to see if any more visitors are allowed. I think she has more than what's permitted already."

The woman picked up the phone to dial Sheryl's room. Meanwhile Leslie was steady talking.

"We've been driving for four hours coming from L.A. We got lost and everything. We just want to see her and make sure she's all right. We want her to know that we came and that we're concerned," she pled our case.

The woman looked around and then hung the phone back up. "Go ahead," she whispered, reaching her hand out to press a button that was to her right.

Double doors opened outward and Leslie and I trotted through.

We proceeded down the long hall, looking at each room number using them to lead us to Sheryl's. We arrived at her room and with a bit of reservation we walked inside.

"Hello," Leslie greeted the room of people.

"Hi," I was immediately behind her.

The people said hello and looked us over trying to figure out who we were.

"I'm Leslie, a friend of Sheryl's from the Tahiti trip," Leslie extended her hand to everybody.

In the middle of the handshakes, Sheryl's voice sounded, "What are you doing here? The audacity of you to come here."

Everybody's faces frowned at once as they looked back and forth at Sheryl and Leslie.

I quickly positioned myself in front of Leslie hoping that Sheryl would calm down at the sight of me.

"Sheryl," I said, softly and nurturing.

"I don't want her here," she shook her head. Tears gathering in her eyes, she suddenly raised her voice, "YOU'RE THE REASON I'M IN HERE! I ALMOST DIED BECAUSE OF YOU! AND YOU KNOW WHAT ELSE? YOU'RE THE REASON I WILL NEVER WALK AGAIN! GET OUT OF HERE! GET OUT OF HERE!"

The commotion caused everybody to get upset. One woman rushed to Sheryl's aide trying to calm her and keep her at rest. Another was looking at Leslie like she wanted to fight her. And a third woman was asking us to go.

Leslie was frozen, her face beet red. She was obviously distraught. I had to basically drag her out of the room. It was either I do it or at some point Sheryl's family would have done it for me.

Out in the hall, a tall, slender, light brown-skinned girl came running after us.

"Are you Angie?" she asked.

I turned around. "Yes."

"I'm Ramona, the one you called earlier."

"Oh, hi," I said. "I'm sorry all this happened. We just wanted to come show our support for Sheryl," I explained.

"What happened today? Why did she go off on her?" Ramona referenced an apparently traumatic Leslie.

"It's a long story, Ramona. And speaking for Leslie right now I'm sure she'd like to tell you her side of it some day soon. But right now, I think I should just get her home."

"Okay, well you have my number, please call me."

"I will," I said, grabbing Leslie by her arm and guiding her out of the automatic doors.

We left the hospital in less time than it took us to park and find Sheryl's room. I opted to drive, seeing as though Leslie was in a trance-like state. I set the navigation to my house. I figured Leslie might as well spend the night. It had been one hell of a day for each of us and all I wanted was for it to be over.

Leslie

"*I KNOW THE REASON WHY YOU KEEP PUTTING YOUR HANDS ON ME! AND IT HAS NOTHING TO DO WITH ME!*" *my mom hollered at no one in particular as she opened and closed various kitchen cabinets, grabbing bottles of liquor from certain ones.* "*THIS IS THE PROBLEM! NOT ME! THIS IS WHAT MAKES YOU BEAT ON ME! IT'S NOT ANYTHING I DO!*" *she went on, pouring bottle after bottle out into the sink.*

My brother and I were at the top of the stairs lying on our stomachs with our elbows propped up and our heads resting in our palms. We were watching our mother go on a crazy rampage after one of her routine beatings by our father. Our baby sister was in her crib, I hoped asleep.

Amused by the dramatic outpouring of our father's stash of alcohol, my brother and I watched on as if we were looking at a movie. This was the first time we had seen our mother throw such a fit. I think it was even the first time either of us had heard her raise her voice. I mean, we had heard her scream before, but for help not out of anger.

In the midst of my mother emptying what must've been bottle number seven, my father came storming in the kitchen door.

"*WHAT THE HELL ARE YOU IN HERE DOING?*" *he asked, a monstrous look on his face.*

Chills traveled down my spine at my father's entrance. I don't think any of us expected him back

179

home so soon. Usually he didn't come in until hours after he'd give my mother a good beating.

My mother stopped in her tracks. She turned around frightened. Her back pressed against the sink and a half empty bottle of rum in her hand, she cried, "I'M SORRY, DANNY --"

My father instantly reached out and wrapped both his hands around my mother's frail neck, the force causing her feet to dangle off the floor.

My brother jumped up from the lying position he was in and attempted to dart down the stairs. I guessed to help save our mother. But I grabbed him by his arm and restrained him with all my might. At only nine he was too young to understand that had he gone downstairs and tried to intervene, he probably would have died alongside our mother. Four years his senior, I knew better. I was trying to spare him.

Meanwhile, we witnessed our father use his steel-toe work boots to kick our mother repeatedly in her head until no more movement came from her or it.

"Huuhh, huuuhh," I woke up panting, drenched in sweat. I looked around the dark room and couldn't figure out where I was. I got up out the bed and made my way to the light switch. I turned it on and while I waited for my eyes to adjust to the sudden brightness, I peered around the room. The African figurines and paintings reminded me that I was at Angie's.

I walked to the bathroom attached to the guest room. I turned on the light. Standing over the sink, I looked at myself in the mirror. I turned on the faucet and splashed the cold water on my face several times. Grabbing a towel from a wicker basket that sat atop a spa bench against the wall, I patted my face dry. I used the same towel to absorb the sweat that covered my neck and chest. Then tossing it into a matching wicker laundry basket, I turned the light out and went back into the bedroom.

I sat on the edge of the bed. My mind was filled with thoughts of my mom's murder, Sheryl choking me at the prison, Kenneth taking my child, Angie being the person whose house my brother had broken into and Sheryl screaming at me from her hospital bed that I was who was responsible for her being paralyzed. I was overwhelmed with emotion. I couldn't stay still. I stood up and paced the room, peeping out the windows, the door, and going back and forth to the bathroom. There was no way I would be able to fall back asleep.

I decided to leave Angie's and go home. At least there I could get to my sleeping pills. I slipped my dark denim skinny jeans on, removed the oversized Barnes' Family Reunion T-shirt that Angie had given me to sleep in and replaced it with my white cotton and lace Free People tank and stepped into my leopard Louboutin peep-toe pumps. I grabbed my pocketbook from out of the modern sleek recliner chair in the corner and left out the room.

I tiptoed down the hall to avoid waking Angie. I got to her front door, opened it slowly and crept out. I got in my car that was parked in the circular driveway outside Angie's front door, started it up and drove off.

The whole way to my condo in the Hollywood Hills, I was thinking about how strange it was that Sheryl, Angie and myself were connected in so many deep-rooted ways. It was one thing that we all were seeing Dr. Anna and ended up not only on the same flight but sitting next to one another going to Tahiti. But the fact that Sheryl was Kenneth's wife, and Angie was Danny's victim, was a whole other story.

Lisa Wu Hartwell
and Miasha

I couldn't help but wonder about the irony. And as I tried over and over to come up with a rational explanation I found myself doing something I hadn't done since my mother's passing—and that was asking God for help.

Sheryl

It had been two weeks since the accident and my hospitalization. But it felt like years. Everyday it was the same thing. Respiratory therapy in the morning, which consisted of deep-breathing exercises and chest percussions. Followed by my routine position change by my physical therapist to prevent bedsores. After that it was stretching of my limbs to maintain flexibility, and strengthening exercises for the muscles that still had some movement. Later I'd be evaluated by my occupational therapist whose goal was to increase my sitting tolerance and balance. And, of course, by evening I was in front of a psychiatrist whose job it was to help combat the depression that understandably came with my injury and get me to focus on attainable goals for myself and my recovery.

By nightfall, I was in my room, alone or sometimes accompanied by one or two visitors who would sit with me, play a game of checkers or UNO until visiting hours were over. Then it was off to sleep with hopes and dreams of waking up to a new day only to find that the one before was just a nightmare.

"Knock, knock," a person's voice accompanied the knocking on my room door.

I was sitting up in the bed eating ice cream when in walked Dr. Anna and Angie carrying a vase full of beautiful fresh flowers, cards, and a bundle of *Get Well* balloons.

It put a smile on my face. "Wow," I said. "What a surprise."

"Hi, Sheryl." Dr. Anna walked over to me and leaned forward to kiss me on my cheek.

Angie was right behind her with a follow-up kiss. "How are you feeling today?" she asked.

"Better now," I said, looking at the pink and white flowers as Dr. Anna sat them in the windowsill. "I love lotuses."

"So we've been told," Angie commented.

She took a seat on the edge of my bed while Dr. Anna sat in the chair diagonally across from us. I finished up my vanilla ice cream and sat the empty cup on the bed tray beside me.

Still smiling I said, "Thank you guys. You just brightened my day."

"Awww," Angie sighed. "I'm glad."

Dr. Anna just smiled. "It's good to finally see you, Sheryl," she said.

"I know," Angie agreed.

For the past two weeks after I had lashed out at Leslie I opted not to have visits from anybody other than family. Trying to come to terms with my disability, I didn't have it in me to deal with anything else, especially not the drama and memories of what happened between Leslie and me. So when I had gotten calls from Angie and Dr. Anna asking if they could come see me, I respectfully told them "Not now." I let them know that I would reach out to them when I was ready to see them. They understood and it wasn't until yesterday I called Dr. Anna and told her it was all right for them to come up. I didn't know they would come the very next day, but I was pleased.

"So, how have you been?" Angie asked.

I shook my head and replied, "Just been, you know. What more can I say?"

"Well I see you've been eating," Dr. Anna joked, referencing my obvious weight gain.

"It's the steroids, Dr. Anna," I playfully corrected her.

"Do they have you moving around at all?" she asked.

I nodded. "Everyday for most of the day," I told her. "It's nerve wrecking, though."

"Why?" Angie was curious. "I would think laying in bed all day would be nerve wrecking."

"Well, when you were so used to doing something without a single thought and that ability is suddenly taken away, it gets frustrating."

"Oh, I see," Angie said.

"I mean, getting up and walking was second nature to me. And now . . ." I shrugged my shoulders, "It's something I can't do at all."

"Well I'm just thankful you're still here with us." Dr. Anna reminded me of my greatest blessing. "I'd rather your life change than be taken from you."

"That's true," Angie said.

I understood what they were saying and I had my days where I felt the same way, but on other days I felt the exact opposite. Trying to maintain a positive attitude though, I responded, "Yeah, you're right."

"So, what's next for you?" Angie jumped to a new topic. "When do you get out of here?"

"About another two weeks if I continue to show progress then I'll be transferred to a rehabilitation center."

"Is that where they'll get more intense with the physical therapy?" Dr. Anna asked.

"From what I've been told," I said.

"And then from there you'll be able to go home?" Angie asked.

"Yup. Once I learn all the skills necessary to care for myself. I'm just hoping I will before my court date for spousal support. I need that more than anything right now; and if they dismiss it because I'm a no show, I don't know what I'm going to do." I shared a concern of mine that had been weighing heavily on me for some time.

I had been awaiting this hearing since Eric was killed. Before then I could care less about spousal support. Eric had made it clear to both Kenneth and me that I wouldn't need it. He made a deal with Kenneth that if he signed the divorce papers and bowed out gracefully that he wouldn't have to worry about me coming after him for anything. Eric told Kenneth he would take good care of my daughter and me. I believe now that that was what made Kenneth flip.

He realized that I wouldn't need him anymore, and therefore he would lose power and control over me. The type of man he was he couldn't handle that. So the only way for him to get back that control was to take away my financial security, which was Eric. And once that was done, it was to take away my strength, which was my child. He succeeded in both. And now that I was coming close to having to fight to get them back, I was faced with a greater bout -- that of living with paralysis. I wondered how likely it was for me to win all three battles, and often thought it was not likely at all. Was I down for the count or would I somehow, someway, come out of this victorious?

"You will." Dr. Anna's comment on my previous statement was perfectly timed. "And if there's anything I can do to help in that process, you let me know. I know they probably have you set up with a psychiatrist in here, but if you ever want a second opinion or just have the desire to talk to somebody else, you know I'm here."

"That goes for me, too," Angie said. "Anything I can do."

"Thanks, y'all. I appreciate it," I said with a bit of emptiness. Those words were so cliché. And although most people who used them meant them, there was never any real action to back those words up. Thus, I had made up my mind that I was in this fight on my own.

"Annnd," Angie added, "I know you might not want to hear it right now, but Leslie told me to tell you she's here for you, too. You're in her prayers."

I could feel the expression on my face change even though I was trying to maintain a smile. The fact of the matter was hearing Leslie's name made me tinge a little. That was the whole reason I had avoided a visit from Angie and Dr. Anna. I didn't want Leslie's name to come up.

"She sent this card," Angie placed a sealed envelope in my lap. "It has her side of the story. And she told me to tell you that even if after knowing the truth you still prefer to stay clear of her she respects your wishes."

I let the card stay where it was for the duration of Angie and Dr. Anna's visit. I didn't want them to know how upset I was. I didn't want them to feel bad for just trying to help.

The rest of the visit we spent talking and laughing about specific memories from Tahiti. I brought up how shocked I was when Dr. Anna had us stuffing dollar bills down strippers' g-strings, telling people who had hurt us to suck it. Angie commented on how drunk the two of us had gotten on the first day and that prompted me to bring up the cursing out I had received from her jealous girlfriend.

"Oh, that bitch turned out to be beyond crazy," Angie laughed.

Dr. Anna and I followed suit. The hours winded down and it was time for Dr. Anna and Angie to leave. And when they did I was in a much better mood than I had been in before they had come.

I was all set to go to sleep when I noticed the card from Leslie was still on my lap. I wasn't going to open it, but I was curious to know her side of the story. After all, for nine years I wondered what was on the mind of the woman who had given birth to my daughter. Now I was finally able to find out.

Angie

I had bottles of Merlot, Moscato, Reisling and Sangria and a few butlered hors d'oeuvres. My guests were in attendance, Leslie, Ramona and the two district attorneys who had been assigned to prosecute Daniel Caruso, Leslie's brother and my thought-to-be stalker.

After allowing some time for them to get familiar with each other, sip their choice of red or white wines, and munch on quesadillas and spring rolls, I asked for their attention.

"First of all, I want to thank you for coming here this evening," I started off. "You all know that I called you here to help out someone who is dear to me and to some of you as well. Here's the thing, a friend of mine, Sheryl Lee, is in the hospital right now recovering from a spinal injury she got in a car accident. Now, I just had the opportunity to meet this woman a little over two weeks ago and it feels like I've known her my whole life. She has experienced one tragedy after the other since marrying her ex-husband Kenneth, who is now incarcerated for killing her fiancé three months ago."

The looks on my guests' faces were serious and sympathetic as they took in all of what I was saying. "Now without getting into too much detail, I want to help her get her life back on track. And I called each of you here because I know that you can help me do that in some way."

I began to delegate. "First of all, she has a court hearing coming up in a month. That's where you come in, Jerry and Thomas." I nodded toward the older, stout, white-haired attorneys. "I know you two were supposed to represent me in the stalker situation but that has changed. I am not going to move forward with that and I will let you know why when it's just us."

The D.A.s were obviously baffled. They looked at each other then back at me, one pushing his glasses to the back of the bridge of his nose and the other brushing his palm over his hair. "But, I will need you to let me know what your retainer will be to represent Sheryl in her spousal support case. I'll give you the details of that in a second."

"Ramona," I looked over at Sheryl's best friend, who was seated on the far end of my handcrafted chenille and ivory sectional. "You told me that the day Sheryl got into her accident the two of you went to the Department of Family and Child services to see about getting her daughter back, right?"

"Yes," Ramona said.

"Well I'm going to need you to tell Leslie which location it was."

Leslie raised her hand to let Ramona know who she was and Ramona blurted out, "The one she went off on? Why would I give her that information?"

"Leslie will explain it to you since it seems Sheryl hasn't already," I told Ramona and kept it moving.

"Now, the goal is to take care of all of this in time for Sheryl's hearing. It is the one thing she is worried most about right now and I want us to alleviate her of that worry. Does anyone have any questions?" I looked at the four of them. After a brief hesitation they all shook their heads. "Good."

I then instructed Leslie and Ramona to exchange telephone numbers while I sat with the district attorneys to break down the complete story as to why I was no longer going through with prosecuting Daniel.

After that, my focus was on Kenneth and all the possible ways we could make him pay -- both literally and metaphorically. *Bastard.*

**Lisa Wu Hartwell
and Miasha**

Leslie

I went straight home and tore my condo apart looking for my daughter's keepsakes box I had purposely hidden from myself. I looked high and low, in boxes, bins, closets, and drawers.

Flashbacks of my mother searching our kitchen cabinets for my father's vices tried to distract me but I wiped them out my mind as I was determined to find my daughter's birth certificate. That, and a picture ID, was all I needed to talk to a social worker down at the Department of Child and Family Services.

I got to the linen closet and after pulling just about every sheet, towel, and blanket off the shelves my eyes were drawn to a safe on the top shelf. Standing on my toes, I reached my arm up as far as I could. It was still out of reach. I left the closet and went into the kitchen where I retrieved a stepladder from the pantry. I took the stepladder into the hallway over to the linen closet and used it to get me the height of the top shelf.

I pulled the safe down slowly and carefully and stepped off the ladder. I sat there on the floor in the hall, the safe in front of me, turning the combination lock. The code came to me instantly upon seeing the safe. It was my daughter's birthday.

I opened it up and inside was a small pink princess box with a hospital-taken photo of my newborn when she was only days old inserted in the tiny frame that was built in the box's lid.

I picked up the box and stared at the picture, dragging my finger up and down my baby's face. A teardrop falling onto it, I wondered what had become of my little girl. Was she happy or sad? Smiling or Crying? And I needed to know badly.

I opened the box and took the birth certificate along with the hospital discharge paper and other forms of proof that she had belonged to me, just in case I should need it.

I closed the box back up and put it back into the safe. It was late, about eleven o'clock, the time I normally went to bed. But excited and nervous I was unable to sleep. I decided to clean my entire house of the mess I made searching for what I had left of my long-lost daughter.

Sheryl

"You can do it," my therapist encouraged. "Just use your arms for support," she said, watching intensely as I gripped the arms of the wheelchair. "And lift!" she cheered as I used all the strength I had to push my butt up from the wheelchair only to fall right back down.

"That's okay, that's okay," she affirmed. "We'll try again."

I was tired of trying though. It was frustrating me. Time after time, I would lift and fall. It was getting redundant; discouraging actually. It was as if the disability was playing tricks on my mind making me believe that maybe I could do it, maybe I could stand up, and eventually maybe I could walk again. Then it would debilitate me and remind me that none of that would ever happen again. I was over it.

"Why don't you just let me get used to living life from this wheelchair?" I asked my therapist.

She knelt down, put her hand on my knee and started delivering some sort of inspirational message that I had completely tuned out. I was more attentive to the fact that her hand was resting on my knee and I couldn't feel it there. And it was little things like that that angered me more. Had my eyes been closed I would have never known her hand was there. And just to make sure that was correct, I closed my eyes.

"Sheryl," my therapist said. "Are you listening to me?"

I squeezed my eyes shut hoping that I would feel something. Then seeking one last hope I asked, "Is your hand still on my knee?"

"Yes," she said. "Do you want me to move it?"

I opened my eyes and wiped them of the tears that started to develop. Manually turning the wheels on my chair I turned away from my therapist. I wheeled out of the exercise room down the hall and into my room.

I no longer wanted to be bothered. And like always when I had gotten to that point, my therapist let me be. She didn't attempt to get me to come back and finish our session. Instead, she sent a message through my nurse that I did well today and she'd see me next time.

In one ear and out the other the message went, which was becoming just as redundant as my so-called recovery.

Today was truly one of my bad days, I thought as I pushed the power button on the TV remote. A black and white picture appeared on the screen. I recognized the scene from the classic movie *Annie*. "Tomorrow, tomorrow, I love you tomorrow," I whimpered to the tune of one of America's most popular theme songs.

"I hope so," I muffled, speaking of my feelings toward tomorrow. "I hope so."

**Lisa Wu Hartwell
and Miasha**

Angie

*B*imp, BImp, BIMp BIMP... my alarm clock gradually reached it's loudest, startling me into jumping from my sleep.

I reached over and turned it off. The time was seven o'clock. The last time I had gotten up that early was in Tahiti a month and a half ago. I stretched, tossed and turned and stretched some more, hoping all of that would help me get out of the bed.

Today was the moment of truth -- Sheryl's court date. We had to be at the courthouse at nine. I called Leslie to make sure she was up. She said she was in the sauna in her condo building's gym. Apparently she had been up an hour already. I called Ramona. She was getting into the shower as we spoke. Lastly, I called Dr. Anna who was showing up merely as moral support, and because she lived quite a distance away and would likely run into rush-hour traffic, she was already on the road.

Everybody was on point. I got up and headed straight for the shower. After washing, I wrapped myself in a towel. I brushed my teeth, flossed, and then moisturized my body and face. Afterward, I applied my makeup. I shook my locks and rubbed my fingers through them to create some sort of style. Then I put on a pair of panties and matching bra and walked down the hall to the laundry room. I covered the rest of my body in a black suit and off white blouse that I had hung on the steamer the night before.

I walked back to my room and into my walk-in shoe closet. I searched out a pair of simple black Gucci stilettos. I paired them with a black Gucci hobo and headed out the door.

A driver was waiting promptly at my gate. I buzzed him in and waited on the front step for him to get down my driveway. I would have drove myself but I didn't want to have to worry about parking.

"Good morning," the tall, solid, body-guard-type driver greeted me as he opened the back door for me.

"Good morning," I said, sliding onto the black butter-soft leather seats.

As we made our way onto the interstate, butterflies made their way into my stomach. I hoped for a victorious outcome, as any more devastation was sure to take Sheryl to the brink.

Leslie

I was so antsy picking my brother up from my grandma's. I had smoked like three cigarettes just waiting for him to figure out how to tie his tie.

"You ready?" I asked at the sight of him walking away from the mirror that hung on the wall in my grandma's dining room.

"Yeah, how do I look?" he asked, adjusting the Windsor knot one final time.

"You look good baby brother," I told him, looking him over. "You should apply for a job at Brooks Brothers after this," I joked while following him out the door.

We got into my car and my brother turned to me. "Thank you sis," he said.

Turning the key in the ignition I asked, "For what?"

"For holding me back all those years ago." He started to choke up. "I know you held on to a lot of guilt for that, wishing you would have not only let me go to help mama but would have ran down there and helped her yourself," he somehow tapped into thoughts of mine that were buried deep in my brain. "You saved our lives. And you should carry pride around for that, not guilt," he concluded.

I didn't say anything, although I humbly appreciated him taking the time to tell me that. For so long I had thought he was mad at me for not letting him go defend our mother. I even blamed myself when he got strung out, and I catered to his every need as much as I could out of guilt. I was sure he knew that, too, and took advantage of it. But it was good to see him come clean about how he really felt. It was a step toward him taking responsibility for himself rather than continuing to put that burden on me. In my mind, that meant he was ready for change. Maybe now he would clean himself up and live right, I hoped. Maybe going to jail was just the awakening that he needed. They say there's a reason for everything. And as the reasons for the craziness that has happened in my life over the past few months continue to unfold, I see that it is all adding up.

Sheryl

I wheeled into the courtroom, my heart in my gut. No legal team with me, just my mom and Ramona. Immediately I spotted Kenneth's team of cold-hearted, money-hungry lawyers. And lurking in the shadows of their power was Kenneth in the same prison uniform I had seen him in forty-five days ago.

As I took my position in the front of the court, I could feel his eyes on me. I glanced over, just to see what type of reaction he'd give to me being wheelchair bound. And like I expected he had a smirk on his face. He appeared to be amused. I couldn't for the life of me understand how a person who had loved me at one point could have so much hate toward me at another. Especially seeing as though I didn't do anything wrong to him. Maybe he never loved me at all. He couldn't have.

I looked back at Ramona and my mom who were in the row immediately behind the table I was sitting at which was reserved for my counsel and me. Ramona shot me a look of encouragement. My mom, although she tried to appear strong, looked like she just wanted to break down crying.

Within moments the judge appeared and the bailiff asked everybody to rise. Of course I couldn't, and that seemed to amuse Kenneth even more.

The judge addressed the court as he took his seat on the bench. "Are all attorneys present?"

"Yes, we are," one of Kenneth's lawyers responded.

The judge looked to me. "Mrs. Lee, do you have an attorney?"

"I'll be representing my --"

"We are here, Your Honor." A middle-aged white man walked through the doors, followed by another middle aged white man, Angie, and a younger white guy.

I was confused as the team took their places beside me. I looked at Angie and she gave me the thumbs up. Clearly this was her doing.

"Don't worry," the man who sat beside me whispered in my ear. "We're gonna milk him for all he's worth."

"Good morning, judge, please forgive our tardiness. Traffic was unkind, as usual," the other member of my team addressed the judge.

"Good morning, Jerry. Good to see you," the judge said in return.

At that Kenneth's team grew very uncomfortable; at least that's what their facial expressions and body language signaled. And in that instant the tables had turned. I was the one with an amused look on my face and Kenneth was now angry.

"Okay, let's get this show on the road," the judge said nonchalantly. "Do the parties have a stipulated agreement of any sort?"

Kenneth's attorney was about to say something and my attorney cut him off.

"No, they don't, Your Honor. And according to the OSC the opposing party claimed he had no assets or income to be able to pay spousal support. But, Your Honor, I'd like to bring into evidence his million-dollar estate," my attorney said, taking a file full of papers and photos to the judge. "Also, his collection of classic and exotic automobiles, and his standard of living which according to Family Codes 4301 and 4302, have to be taken into consideration --"

"Wait a minute, Your Honor," Kenneth's lawyer spoke up. "This is all nonsense. Our client has been incarcerated for the past three-and-a-half months, during which time he has sold his assets to be able to afford representation and has not generated any income to be able to take care of himself or his child let alone another grown and capable individual."

The judge looked at me then at Kenneth's lawyer, "She doesn't look so capable," the judge noted.

"Yeah, well her condition is new to us," he said. "It could be a ploy for all we know, Your Honor."

"Judge," my attorney now said, "the assets that were sold to supposedly pay for Mr. Stewart's representation, and fine representation, might I add," he threw in some sarcasm, "were sold to members of his family for staggeringly low amounts like," rubbing his goatee, he looked down at a legal pad on top of his briefcase, "twenty-five dollars for a custom built Beverly Hills mansion, fifteen dollars for a two-bedroom penthouse on Medano Beach in Cabo San Lucas. And just two dollars for a 1937 Mercedes Benz 540K Special Roadster, the same car that cost Mr. Stewart approximately four million dollars in 2002."

The judge shot a dirty look at Kenneth and then brought his attention back to my attorney.

"Now, the fact that these amounts are ridiculously low for these types of assets is not even what concerns me, Your Honor. What concerns me is how on earth Mr. Stewart was able to hire this team of fine lawyers for only forty-two bucks."

"Your Honor, can we please approach the bench?" Kenneth's lawyer asked, sweat gathering at his temples.

"I don't see a need to," the judge said, angrily. "Do you have any evidence of these transactions, Jerry?" he asked my attorney.

The one sitting beside me handed Jerry a folder that he had taken from Jerry's briefcase.

"Yes, I do, Your Honor. They're all in there," he gave the judge the file.

"Let me look over these and deliberate. I want you all back here in fifteen." The judge stood up and exited the courtroom.

Shortly afterward, a sheriff took Kenneth to the inmates' holding area and Kenneth's attorneys called my attorneys out into the hall.

"Oh my God," I gasped with excitement. I looked back at Angie. "How did you do this?"

She came to the front along with Ramona and my mom who were both beaming with satisfaction.

"It was a surprise," Ramona squealed. "She called us all to her house and said she wanted to help you."

I shook my head in disbelief. "I don't know what to say. I'm speechless."

"Well, I want to thank you," my mom turned to Angie, putting her hands on top of hers. "You are truly a blessing at a time like this."

Angie proceeded to tell me how she was able to pull the whole thing off. It was a long and twisting story that even included Leslie's brother who was the younger white guy who had come into the courtroom with her and her lawyers.

He introduced himself to me. Apparently, he was there to testify about Kenneth's outlandish spending in prison, which included treating his whole cellblock to pizza twice a week and purchasing the most expensive items from the canteen every visit. I thanked him for his willingness to do such a thing for me, and he expressed,

"After what he did to my sister he's lucky I let him live."

I didn't have time to respond because the judge was making his way back into the court. But what he said moved me. It made me think that maybe Leslie's side of the story was true. After all, I couldn't put it pass Kenneth to do something so egregious. I made a mental note to contact Leslie immediately after court to apologize. I had no idea that I would not have to go far.

The judge ruled in my favor, awarding everything my attorneys had asked for on my behalf -- the house, the cars, and the beach home, plus twenty-thousand dollars a month for me and fifteen thousand dollars a month for our child.

"Hold the fuck up!" Kenneth finally lost his cool. "She don't even have my child!" he protested.

"Yes, she does," a familiar voice came from the back of the courtroom. Everybody's heads turned.

Leslie was walking down the aisle of the court but what my eyes fixated onto was the tall, thin, light yellow girl with hazel eyes and dark blonde hair. I watched her innocently glide down the aisle toward me, and I swore I was dreaming. It seemed the earth stopped spinning and there was no one in the room but her and I.

"Shannon," I whispered as she approached me.

"Mommy!" she squealed, tears streaming down her angelic face.

Without thought, I pushed up on the arms of my wheelchair, lifting myself onto both feet. I hugged my little girl tight without falling or even losing balance. "I've been waiting for this for so long," I cried. "Thank you. Thank you. Thank you." I sent my most sincere thanks up to God.

Leaving the courtroom with all three of my battles won, I realized that I had finally had my breakthrough. I might not have gotten it back in Tahiti at the dress burning ceremony like the other women had, but I had gotten it now.

I had awakened from a thirteen-year plus nightmare and now would begin living my dreams with newfound hope, strength, and friendships to last me a lifetime.

Lisa Wu Hartwell
and Miasha

Excerpt from the book
'*Til Death*
by Miasha
(Available in Bookstores Nationwide!)

"WHAT ABOUT THE SO-CALLED PACT WE HAD? HUH? WHAT HAPPENED TO THAT? 'TIL DEATH, REMEMBER?" I screamed at Si-Si.

"THIS IS DEATH!" she yelled back, then she paused. She looked around as if she was trying to see if our outbursts were bringing any unwanted attention our way. Then she took a second to gather her composure. "Death to Sienna, death to Si-Si, death to Vida," she said in a much lower tone.

"What are you talkin' about Si-Si?" I asked, too frustrated and too high to figure out any riddles.

"The life we were living is over, Celess. It's a wrap. Give it up. Turn yourself in. The streets are not safe for you," she demanded.

"And they're safe for you?" I asked. "What, you want me to cover my whole body? Will that make me safe? 'Cause if that's what you want, I'll do it. But I'm not turning myself in!" I said. "Not unless you are!" I added.

"Well that's your choice," she gave no argument. "Whatever you decide to do that's on you."

"Okay, cool. Now that we have that understanding, what are you going to do? I say we hook with some of these rich-ass oil niggas and build us an empire off they dime," I wanted bad to get back the life Si-Si and I had when it was good.

"I'm done with all that, Celess," Si-Si shook her head. "Last night," she began slowly and steadily as if the words that were about to come off her tongue were fragile. "Amir took me to take my shahada. Then this morning we went...and got married."

I was in total and utter shock, almost speechless but I was able to yell out, "WHAT?!"

Si-Si looked around again. Then she explained, "Celess, I don't wanna end up like my mom," tears began to escape her light brown eyes, which was all I could see of her. "Or like all the other women I've known throughout my life. I *want* to grow old someday. I wanna settle down and have children, watch them grow and play and laugh and learn and just witness a normal existence before I leave this earth. And I don't see that happening if I continue on this path. All the sex, and the drugs, the alcohol, and the partying, it's all a waste," she said shaking her head. "Wasted energy, wasted money, wasted time. I mean, we had our fun, yes, I'll admit that. But realistically," she paused, looked down and back up then she continued, "how long will it last?" Si-Si wiped her eyes and took a breath. She shrugged her shoulders and with the most sincere look in her eyes she said, "I want a *real* life, Celess, not just a fast one."

Too bad I wasn't buying it. I mean, not only was it sudden and random like many decisions Si-Si made.

But I was high and she was blowin' it. I rolled my eyes and folded my arms, resting them across my stomach. I was so ready to dismiss all that Si-Si was saying. I mean, we had been through so much shit together and for her to just turn her back on me for some nigga she practically just met didn't make any sense to me. I was sure she was just talking out her ass. Amir got in her ear a little bit, broke her off some good dick and flashed his wealth before her and she was ready to submit. I was sure she just needed a wake-up call.

"We're still young, Si-Si! You actin' like we 'bout to croak! We have our whole lives to change," I reminded her, thinking about the ten years minimum that we had left to play with.

Si-Si didn't say anything. She just looked around, her eyes bouncing off one golden dome rooftop to the next. I thought I had her and I started to seal the deal with a plan for us to both switch out of the fast lane in 2014. I figured we could agree to at least five more years of making money and moves. But right before I had the chance to propose we make a deal, she said something that sent chills down my spine.

"Celess, you need to get out of the game while you still *have* your life to change."

I unfolded my arms and brought my hands to my face holding them over my eyes for a second. The last time I heard someone say something like that to me, I didn't take heed. And not only did I come close to death but I also lost the dearest person to me.

I had mixed emotions. I didn't know what to say or do, but right then on that rooftop in Dubai, my life with Si-Si up until that moment flashed before my eyes like scenes from an action movie. Taking me back to the beginning, fifteen months ago when she and I first stepped off the plane in Rome.

October 2007

"I got a million text messages," Si-Si said as soon as her phone booted up.

"You too?" I said, glancing down at my phone as I briskly walked beside her through the Leonardo Da Vinci Airport headed toward baggage claim. It was a quarter after four. We had been in the air for close to 16 hours since we departed Los Angeles the day before. The Rome airport was extra crowded for some reason. I mean, yes it was a Friday and I'm sure that had a lot to do with there being lots of travelers but goodness there had to be another reason for the massive amount of people entering Rome on that day.

"David is worried sick," Si-Si said of the famous Hollywood actor she fell in love with several months back. "He's like, 'call me please. They're saying your either dead or running from the law…'" she whispered one of the many messages she had on her phone.

I looked at her as she scrolled her Dash with the same pity in my eyes that she had in her voice and I huffed. I knew it had to be hard on her abruptly leaving David and then not being able to let him know she was safe.

"I wish I could call him of all people," she continued. "Just to tell him I'm okay."

Like I figured, I thought. I didn't say anything but it was a good thing that Si-Si read my silence correctly and she didn't call.

"I just think we need to get somewhere safe before we decide what we're goin' to do and who we're goin' to call."

Si-Si nodded in agreement. "You're right," she said. "We gotta be smart."

"Everything we do and say gotta be thought-out," I added. I looked at Si-Si for her response and she nodded again although she didn't seem to be paying me much attention anymore. Instead, she was focused on the crowd of people standing before us holding signs up for whomever they were there to pick up.

"Where is Andrew?" she mumbled, her eyes squinting.

"Call him," I said.

"Damn it!" she exclaimed. "I was supposed to call him as soon as we landed so he could meet us at baggage claim," she said, throwing one hand on her forehead, while the other palmed her phone. Then she mumbled, "All those texts threw me off. And that message from David…"

Si-Si was shaken up I could tell. I never seen her so disoriented before. I decided to take charge. It was clear to me that she was overwhelmed.

"Here, you sit down and call Andrew," I led her to a bench. "I'll go get your bags."

Si-Si did as I told her and she took a seat. Even sitting she couldn't keep still. Her legs were trembling. I watched her for a moment before walking over to the luggage carousel and turned to check on her often. I felt the need to keep a close eye on her. She seemed so unstable. I imagined she was still shook up about having killed that guy back home. And how could I blame her?

No sooner than the carousel began dishing the bags out, did Si-Si's luggage fall onto the belt. *The beauty of first class*, I thought. I reached out to grab them as they got near and a gentleman beat me to them.

"Thank you, sir," I said as I reached out to accept the bags from him. He was a medium height white guy with some edge and even a little bit of swagger. He had on a fresh pair of blue, green and white D squared sneakers, a matching V-neck long sleeve Tee, and a pair of True Religion jeans. His dark curly hair peeked through a navy True Religion Trucker hat.

"Are you with Sienna?" he asked without releasing the luggage.

"Sienna?" I questioned, briefly mesmerized by his sexiness. Then a light bulb went off in my head and I said, "Oh yes, Si-Si." Then I followed up, "You must be Andrew."

"Yes," he said, nodding. "And you are?" he looked bewildered.

"Celess," I shook the hand he freed up for our formal introduction. "Si-Si's friend," I added, now wondering if Si-Si even told him about me.

"Oh, I'm sorry," he said, "Si-Si didn't mention to me that she was bringing someone. But, it's certainly nice to meet you."

"Oh," I paused. "Well I hope it's not a problem."

"No, not at all. Do you have bags that I need to get as well?"

I shook my head. "No…I…they lost my luggage," I made up real quick. I sure wasn't about to tell him I had no time to bring my luggage because I was running for my life.

"So, where is Sienna?" he asked anxiously. "I'm dying to see that girl."

"She's actually tryin' to call you," I said, as I led him away from the carousel and over toward where Si-Si was sitting. "We thought we'd be waiting a little while for you to get here seeing as though Si-Si was supposed to call you as soon as we touched down."

"Oh, well, she called when you guys boarded and told me everything was on time so… I actually got here earlier than I planned so I just parked. Figured I'd get her bags and have them waiting for her when she got off the plane," he explained, briskly walking one step behind me.

"Si-Si!" I called out.

She looked up in my direction. Her eyes were locked on me until I got closer to her. They then drifted past me and landed on Andrew.

"Andrew!" she squealed as she stood up to hug him.

He chuckled as he let go of her suitcases to squeeze her in his arms.

"Well looky here," Andrew said, standing back to look Si-Si over. "Where have you been Sienna? What have you been doing?"

Si-Si looked at him, almost staring. Her eyes were watery. She shrugged her shoulders and said, "Just…living." Then she cracked a huge smile as if to keep from crying.

Andrew smiled as well, "Yeah? Well I hope living good."

"As good as life gets," she replied.

"Good," he said. "What brings you to my side of the world? It's been so many years. I thought you forgot about me," Andrew continued, standing stiff as if paralyzed by Si-Si's presence.

"I could never forget you, Andrew," Si-Si said, "Just been trying out independence, that's all."

"How you like it?"

"It's good. It's good. Just can get awfully lonely."

"So you missed me?"

"That's one of the reasons I'm here."

"What would be another?" Andrew prolonged.

"Just needed a change of scenery. One's own world can get so redundant. It never hurts to put it on pause and visit someone else's."

Si-Si had a way with words. I swear she had more game than me.

"Well, let's go. I have a lot of things planned for us," Andrew finally ended the small talk.

"I hope the first thing involves gettin' a drink. Because I need one," Si-Si said.

"Oh, where I'm taking you, there will be champagne for days, my friend."

"And where might that be?" Si-Si asked.

"To Genoa, the biggest boat show in the world. You came at the perfect time," Andrew told her as he grabbed her hand and started to lead us out of the airport.

"Um, wait a minute, my bags," Si-Si reminded Andrew of her luggage that he had let go of minutes ago to greet her.

He shook his head. "Leave them," he said. "Whatever's in them won't stand up to what they have at the shops in Via XX Settembre, believe me. Besides, they won't fit in my car. In fact, we're gonna have to squeeze your friend in. I didn't know you weren't coming alone."

"Oh yeah, that was my fault," Si-Si said. "I had so much going on you wouldn't believe and I just was so happy to get in touch with you, it completely slipped my mind to tell you I was bringing Celess. I hope that's no problem."

Andrew grinned, "Nothing's a problem when you're with me," he told her. "You know that," he put his arm around her shoulder and guided her outside.

In that moment Si-Si lit up. Her whole energy changed. She went from being frazzled and a bit lost to seeming whole again. I guessed she felt a sense of security with her old friend. And when we got outside to his car I could see why.

This handsome Italian guy led us to a white Bugatti Veyron with red leather interior and white piping. The only time I had ever seen one was in an issue of the Robb's Report a while back. The picture did it no justice. It was to die for. If we were going to be stuck on another continent for who knew how long I was soooo happy and relieved to know that we would be staying with money. Hell, I felt secure too.

Si-Si glanced back at me with a grin on her face. We made eye contact but that was it. We both remained silent as we lapped it in the passenger seat of the 1.4 million dollar car.

We pulled up to yet another airport where a private plane was waiting for us. At first, I figured Andrew had chartered it but after getting on board and seeing his signature engraved in all of the headrests I knew he actually owned the aircraft. Impressive. *Si-Si called the right one*, I thought. My problems back home were fading away faster than I thought they could. And I wondered for a minute was it normal for someone to be so obsessed with money and fine things to the point that nothing else in the wide world mattered. But hell, I never was considered normal in the first place. So why worry about fitting that description now?

"So how long's this flight?" Si-Si asked Andrew as she helped herself to a glass of white wine.

"It's just over 200 miles. We'll be on the ground in no time."

"Well, good, because I'm so over being in the sky right now."

"I bet," Andrew said taking a seat beside Si-Si.

As soon as he sat down, Si-Si rested her head on his shoulder. I watched the two and admired the Kodak moment. Moreover I felt happy for Si-Si. I knew she was distraught about having seen her mother murdered and then having to pull the trigger on a man. I could only imagine what emotions she was feeling. I was just glad that she had someone in addition to me to lean on. Especially, someone as rich as Andrew.

When we landed in Genoa and got off the plane, Andrew led us to another white Bugatti with red leather interior and white piping. It was exactly like the one we had left in Rome. I took a double take.

Si-Si shot Andrew a look like she was thinking the same thing I was and Andrew explained himself.

"I like what I like," he said.

Boy oh boy, I thought, this guy was stuntin' hard and I couldn't help but be turned on by him. Nevertheless I maintained my composure. He was Si-Si's friend. Besides I was sure he had someone he could hook me up when that time came. And what I was even surer about was the fact that whoever that might be had the same type of money Andrew obviously had. Everybody knows birds of a feather flock together. So I would be patient.

We positioned ourselves in the passenger seat again and were off. I hoped we weren't in for a long ride because sitting on Si-Si's lap in the two-seater was uncomfortable. The one thing I did enjoy though was being able to see the sights. Italy was a beautiful place—refreshing even. I mean, the architecture on the buildings there made me want to cry. Honestly, I had never seen anything so unique and prestigious. I thought about my best friend, Tina, and the time she visited Derek's family in Italy during their month long honeymoon and I remembered her telling me how beautiful this country was. She was so right. Quickly I changed the subject in my head. It had been years since Tina was killed, but thinking about her was bound to have me break out into tears. And God knows, I didn't want to do that in front of Andrew. He had just met me not even an hour ago and I didn't want his first impression of me to be that I was this emotional, crazy chick. I turned my attention to the amazingly beautiful vehicle I was in.

After admiring every detail from the navigation screen in the rear-view mirror to the key, which resembled a small pocketknife, I decided to break the silence.

"How much is on the dash?" I asked Andrew.

Without taking his eyes off the spiraling road, he replied, "A little over 250."

"Wow," I said.

Quickly glancing at me, he boasted, "And it gets there in less than a minute."

I nodded my head slowly and repeated, "Wow."

"So what does one have to do to get a car like this?"

"Well, place an order."

"And what's that process?"

"Just 350,000 U.S.D," he said, nonchalantly.

"Three hundred and fifty thousand dollars is needed just to place the order?" I had to verify.

Andrew nodded. "Pretty much."

Even Si-Si commented on that one.

"So where other guys are buying Bentleys or Ferraris Andrew here is using that money just to order his car," she boosted his already big ego. "Gotta love it," she concluded.

"Got to," I added.

After about a quick ten-minute drive from the Genoa Airport we arrived at the Bentley Hotel, a modern luxurious structure with the perfect name. The valet parker was at our door instantaneously.

"Mr. Coselli," the guy nodded his hello to Andrew.

Andrew put some folded bills in his palm and patted him on the shoulder as he made room for him to take his place in the driver seat.

We went inside the 5-star hotel and the lobby reminded me of one of Vegas' most upscale spots. The art deco meets couture décor gave a rich and futuristic feel. We checked into the room Andrew had reserved. Good thing it was a suite because I had my own room. I could enjoy my privacy and Si-Si and Andrew could enjoy theirs. I didn't have any bags or anything so I didn't have much settling in to do. All I did upon entering the luxurious bedroom was come out of my dirty clothes, take a nice long bath, cover up in the complimentary bathrobe and plop down on the bed. I attempted to watch some TV but the language barrier and my exhaustion made that impossible. I was asleep in no time.

I awakened to the smell of hot breakfast, despite the fact it was already lunchtime. Indeed I had slept well into the next day. My body needed the rest. I stretched and got up out the bed. I went to the bathroom washed my face and brushed my teeth. Then I went into the living room to see where the aroma of bacon and eggs was coming from.

"Good afternoon," Andrew said as he ate his pretty well balanced breakfast. He was fully dressed.

"Good afternoon," I said. "I didn't mean to sleep so late. Is Si-Si up and dressed too?"

"No, she's out like a light," he said, focusing on getting a piece of his omelet on his fork. "She didn't sleep well last night. Tossed and turned a lot," he said.

"Oh," I said, "She had trouble sleeping on the plane too."

"Yeah, that's flying commercial for you," he said then he asked, "You want breakfast? There's plenty in there. I figured I'd order everything on the menu rather than wake you two."

"Thank you," I said, "I'm starving," I admitted, going toward the food display.

Andrew wasn't exaggerating. He really did buy the entire menu. Once again I was impressed. He was continuously outdoing himself. He was his own competition. *That's a rich nigga for you*, I thought.

"So Celess, right?" Andrew decided to strike up a conversation.

"Yes."

"You and Sienna were both big actresses in the U.S. huh?"

"Well we were certainly working on it," I said, modestly.

"I see. That's interesting. The last time I saw Sienna she was this young ambitious girl with so much drive and passion. I knew she would go on to do big things."

"Yeah, that's exactly how she was when I met her," I said, recalling the day I was shopping at the boutique Si-Si worked in and how she quit on the spot after I told her I could show her how to get money. I smirked at that memory. To this day I had never met somebody so fearless.

"Well, today is the first day of Salone Nautico Internazionale…"

"The what?" I interrupted Andrew.

"The International Boat Show. It's an annual thing. They showcase some of the biggest and best Yachts."

"Oh right. I remember, yes of course."

"Yeah. And uh, I have my eye on something so I need to be there." He glanced at his watch. "I'm going to leave some money so when sleeping beauty awakes you two can have a driver take you to Via XX Settembre to get some clothes and things. It's within meters of here. You could actually walk but I wouldn't want you to do that. And once you get done call me and I will meet up with you. Okay?"

I nodded. "Sure. Thanks."

Andrew disappeared in the room he and Si-Si shared for a few minutes then he reentered the small living room. He was carrying a wad of cash. I thought he was going to peel a few bills from the wad and hand them to me but he gave me the entire stack.

"Get something nice. I want you two to be the most beautiful girls there. Not that that should be hard. But you know what I mean."

"No worries," I said. "We know how to show up."

Andrew grinned and I took notice at how clean he looked. He wasn't wearing a hat and his hair was slicked back allowing his thick, dark eyebrows to take center stage. *He cleaned up well for the boat show*, I thought. I watched him gather some of his belongings, which included a sports jacket and a briefcase and head out the door. "See you later," he said.

As soon as the door slammed behind him, I started counting the money. There were 575 bills altogether. Two hundred of them said 500 Euros and the other 375 said 200 Euros. That equaled 175,000 Euros. Now what the hell was that in USD? I was anxious to know. I went in the bedroom where Si-Si was oversleeping.

"Si-Si, wake up already!" I started opening the drapes, figuring the bright sunshine would help. "Si-Si!"

"Huuuh?" Si-Si sighed as she slowly rolled over in the bed.

"Wake up girl, ya friend left us a mountain of cash to go shopping and now I can't sit still!"

I sat on the edge of the bed next to Si-Si's head. After rubbing her eyes repeatedly she sat up.

"What?" she asked. "What are you so hype about?"

I waved the money in her face and with a kool-aid smile I said, "this."

"Where did you get that from? Where is Andrew?"

"He left to go to that boat show. He said for us to take this and get something to wear for today. He said he want us to be the baddest bitches at the show."

Si-Si shook her head. "He didn't say that."

"Well not in those exact words but that's what he meant. Now get up, shower and let's go do some damage!"

Si-Si didn't budge. Instead she just shook her head as if to say um um, um.

"What's wrong?" I questioned her lack of enthusiasm.

Then as if she had just snapped out of a daze, she said, "Nothing." And with a more upbeat tone and attitude she said, "Let's go."

It took both Si-Si and I only about a half hour to get dressed. All we had to do was shower and throw on the same clothes from the previous day. We both felt so dirty and uncomfortable but it was only for a short period. We called for car service like Andrew instructed and had the driver take us shopping. It was in the car that Si-Si counted the money for herself. She knew how to convert the currency and everything.

"Two hundred and fifty," she said when she was done.

"You are lying to me!" I couldn't believe that Andrew had given us 250 thousand dollars cash money off the bat.

"No I'm not," Si-Si said. "He's mega rich, Celess. This to him is nothing."

"What the hell, he print money?"

Si-Si chuckled and said, "Something like that."

I paused and looked up at Si-Si, my eyebrows furrowed. I needed clarification. I mean, I wasn't about to be spending no counterfeit money, especially not while I was already running from the law.

"Not like that," she said, reading my thoughts. "He owns stock in the Federal Reserve," she explained. "Lots of it."

"As much as I love money, I don't know what the Federal Reserve is."

"Put it this way," Si-Si broke it down, "He practically owns the US Mint."

"Shit girl! Why the hell we ain't been come out here? Are you kiddin' me?"

She smirked and said, "I told you the money over here was much longer."

"Well I don't know about you, but I ain't never goin' back to the states," I said.

"Never say never," Si-Si quoted.

"You heard me clear bitch, NEVER! Matter fact, how do you say never in Italian?"

We were dropped off in one of the most expensive shopping districts in Genoa. We tipped our driver and hit the pavement headed into Coin, an internationally known designer department store.

"I want the entire window," I said, peeking at the glamorous wares that draped all the mannequins.

Inside, Si-Si and I went from designer section to designer section grabbing everything from lingerie and pajamas to shoes and jackets and everything in between including make-up and perfume. After Coin, it was Streness, a haute-couture boutique near the Carlo Felice Theater. Then it was Fedra, a shop that sold high fashion names like Yves Saint Laurent and Sonia Rykiel. We spent about six hours and just over ninety thousand euros when it was all said and done. We grabbed a late lunch at Zefferino, a famous family-owned restaurant with what had to be the best tasting ravioli in the world.

Afterwards, we hit our driver up to take us back to our hotel where we showered and changed into our new clothes. We both opted to wear Emanuel Ungaro. I was in a sleeveless gray mini-dress with a rock-and-roll type print splashed with red, black, and silver sequins and crystals. I carried a red leather waist-length motorcycle jacket to shield me from the typical by-the-water breeze. On my feet was a pair of red ankle boots by Dior. Si-Si wore a pair of high-waisted royal blue ski pants with a cream strip going down the side of each leg and a gold zipper from the hip to the waist. Tucked into them was a black bodysuit, which she covered with a cropped-sleeve black blazer. On her hands was a pair of cream leather biker gloves. She wore a simple pair of black wedged heeled pumps, also Ungaro.

Andrew was going to get his wish because we were sure to be the best looking girls to ever attend the boat show—in all it's forty something years.

Once we were ready to go Si-Si called Andrew to find out where he wanted us to meet him. He told her to have the driver take us to Porto Antico, which turned out to be around the corner. We didn't know where or what that was but the driver did and that was all that mattered.

We arrived at our destination within minutes. It was a port from which people could take a ferry to Fiera Di Genova, the venue for the boat show. We asked Andrew if he wanted us to take the Ferry and he instructed us to just wait at the port. He would meet us there—and that he did, in a sleek, stainless steel-looking yacht.

At that point I was no longer amazed at Andrew's wealth and how he flaunted it. I stepped onto the powerboat as if it had been my means of transportation for years, with both my head and my nose to the sky. You couldn't tell me anything!

"We're taking a boat to the boat show," Si-Si said as she settled in the passenger seat of the Porsche designed cruiser. "How fitting."

"It's too much road traffic to have come by car," Andrew reasoned with a grin on his face.

He knew road traffic had nothing to do with him picking us up in his 300 thousand dollar watercraft. I mean, we were only minutes away from the convention center. We could've walked in the time it took him to get to the port. He just wanted to stunt like he'd been doing the entire time. I fucked with it, though.

"You look stunning by the way," Andrew complimented Si-Si. "You and Celess both."

"Courtesy of my favorite bachelor," Si-Si replied.

I chimed in, "Yes, all thanks to you."

"Anything for this one," Andrew said, nodding toward Si-Si. "She holds a special place in my heart."

Si-Si blushed and I picked up on a chemistry between the two that I admired. I mean, I could tell Si-

Si was holding back and probably because she was still feeling sorrowfully about her mom and how we left the U.S., which I couldn't blame her for. But I did wish for her to snap out of it. I didn't want her emotions to consume her. I of all people knew how dangerous that could be. I made a mental note to pull her to the side and talk to her about it as soon as we reached land.

"Can I have a minute with Si-Si, please, Andrew?" I asked as he helped me off the boat and onto the marina slip.

Andrew let go of my hand upon me planting my feet on sturdy ground. "Sure," he said. "We have a suite right inside here. Just come on in when you're ready."

"Okay," I nodded. "Thanks."

The minute Andrew disappeared Si-Si turned to me. "What's up?" she asked.

"How are you feeling?" I got to the point.

"Fine," Si-Si said. "Why? What's wrong?"

"Nothing's wrong with me. But you seem to go in and out. And I know we didn't get to really talk about what we were going to do from here so maybe you still feel a little confused or overwhelmed or whatever. But I just want you to know that I'm here for you if you need to talk, get some things off your chest or even if you just need to cry. I don't want you to bottle anything up inside. I want you to be all right."

Si-Si didn't say anything at first. She just looked around. Then after some time she blurted, "Celess, I'm scared. I am so scared."

"I knew it was something," I told her.

"Look," she said, pulling her cell phone from her purse.

I leaned forward to view her screen.

She pulled up a more recent text message from David. It read, *Just need to hear something. Cops found a gun with your prints on it. They're saying you killed a man. What is going on? I'm worried!*

"You text him?" I asked her.

She didn't answer but the look on her face said yes.

"I had to," she confessed. "I had to let him know I was safe and I needed to know what was being said back home."

"You didn't tell him where we were, did you?"

Si-Si shook her head.

I looked out at the endless ocean. The sun was setting beneath the calm waves. The view was breathtaking. I exhaled and turned my attention back to Si-Si.

"Listen," I told her. "I'm not goin' lie, I've been a little worried myself. I mean, I got messages from Ms. Carol, Sean and even Michael all talking about how they seen the murders on the news and that the police were naming us suspects," I confessed about having heard from my shrink and two ex-boyfriends.

Si-Si cut me off, "What are we gonna do, Celess? I mean, should we go back and just turn ourselves in and tell them everything?"

I shook my head. "Hell no. I'm not tryna go to jail."

"But it was self defense. I mean, he was going to kill us. He *killed* my mom." Si-Si looked as if she was going to break down.

"That's true but hard to prove. His back was turned when you shot him. And them twisted laws been done had us both doing time just for protecting our lives. It's too risky."

"Well what, then? We can't stay out here forever."

"Why can't we?" I asked. "You said it yourself, here we can make ten times the money we made back home. So why not stay out here and do just that? I mean, we clearly see it's possible. Look at us, look where we are, what we have on, what we been riding in. It don't get no better than this."

"I know I said that, but that was before what happened to my mom and before what I did. Now, it's different. I feel so hurt and paranoid I can't really enjoy all of this. It's like my mind will only let me escape it for a short while. Then it haunts me all over again."

"I understand. I do. But, with time it will fade, trust me. But you don't wanna be spending that time in nobody's cell constantly reminded of the tragedy that put you there. I don't know about you but I'd much rather be spending that time eating chocolate covered strawberries and sipping champagne on somebody's yacht. You just need time that's all. I say we put the whole thing behind us and act like it never happened."

"Are you okay with that though? I mean, what if they eventually track us down?"

"I say we get rid of our phones. Leave everything that ties us to the past in the past. Leave no traces."

"Are you sure? Because God forbid if that was to happen, if they do catch up to us, you would be in more trouble then than you are now. I don't want to drag you down with me."

"This is my choice, Si-Si. It ain't like you got me up in some third world country shacked up in a hut some damn where. We livin' good and it ain't even been 48 hours yet. Can you imagine what we could be living like with more time to connect and to put some shit together?" I paused briefly. Then I reminded Si-Si, "I told you on the plane after you came clean to me, I'm ridin' and I meant that."

Tears gathered in Si-Si's eyes as she began to take the back of her phone off. "You don't know how much that means to me," she said, removing her sim card from her phone.

I realized what she was doing and followed her lead. I took my cell phone out my purse. I removed my sim card as well. "I say we start over out here as new people with new lives. Hell, if we go back to the states we got everything to lose. Out here, we got everything to gain."

At that Si-Si wiped the tears that seemed determined to break free from her eyes. She raised her arm and threw her phone and sim card out into the sea as if she was pitching for the major leagues. I followed suit. Then we both turned to walk into Andrew's private suite inside the Fiera Di Genova. Italy had no idea what Si-Si and I was about to do to it.

The takeover had officially begun.

Author's Bio – Lisa Wu Hartwell

Lisa Wu Hartwell possesses a grocery list of skills, occupations and accolades. In addition to being everyone's favorite housewife on Bravo's hit reality series *The Real Housewives of Atlanta*, she is many things to many people; A wife, mother, an actress, a writer, a real estate maven, a host, a notorious speed talker and a chronic multi-tasker. Wu Hartwell's activities have all spurred from one interest to another. The bridge that binds her interests together is a vivid curiosity and a can-do attitude that trumped naysayers' negativity.

A love for the arts, Lisa has flourished in the entertainment industry for 15 years, writing and producing plays, such as *Change is Gonna Come*, directed by a then little known director named Tyler Perry; TV shows like UPN's *The Industry*, and movies—one titled, *Black Ball*, in which she starred.

As we can all see, there is more to Lisa Wu Hartwell than meets the eye. Operating with a self-described "ball of energy", she has appeared in an episode of Tyler Perry's "Meet the Browns", is currently working on a film titled *Mo-Ling*, the Gwendolyn Mason story, and is featured in an upcoming Kick-Boxing Workout DVD.

Lisa Wu Hartwell, a Los Angeles native, currently resides outside Atlanta, Georgia with her family.

Author's Bio – Miasha

Having been in the book industry for only four years Miasha has seven novels under her belt, including *Diary of a Mistress*, *Sistah for Sale*, *Mommy's Angel*, *Chaser,* and the *Secret Society* Trilogy. She's captured the attention of major media outlets such as **BET**, **The Wendy Williams Experience**, **CBS**, and **CN8** and has been featured in an array of national magazines from **Essence** to **Vibe Vixen**, including being the first urban literature writer featured in **Elle Magazine**.

Producer of the hit stage play, Secret Society, based on her debut novel, Miasha continues to prove that despite adversities dreams can come true with hard work, determination, and a vision. Secret Society has sold out all of its shows since its opening in July 2008. Diary of a Mistress the Stage Play is next up for this ambitious entrepreneur and she is stopping at nothing to solidify her brand in the theatre and film industries as she has so eloquently done in the publishing industry.

Miasha is the founder of the *Ask Miasha Foundation* geared toward uplifting and empowering underprivileged youth. She resides outside of Atlanta, Georgia with her husband and two children.